ENTER THE WOLF

M. J. CAAN

Vinci Books

vinci-books.com

Published by Vinci Books Ltd in 2026

1

Copyright © M.J. Caan 2018

The author has asserted their moral right to be identified as the author of this work in accordance with the Copyright, Designs and Patents Act 1988. This work is a work of fiction. Names, characters, places and incidents are the product of the author's imagination or are used fictitiously. Any resemblance to actual persons, living or dead, places and incidents is entirely coincidental.

All rights reserved. No part of this publication may be copied, reproduced, distributed, stored in any retrieval system, or transmitted in any form or by any means, including photocopying, recording, or other electronic or mechanical methods, nor used as a source for any form of machine learning including AI datasets, without the prior written permission of the publisher.

The publisher and the author have made every effort to obtain permissions for any third party material used in this book and to comply with copyright law. Any queries in this respect should be brought to the attention of the publisher and any omissions will be corrected in future editions.

A CIP catalogue record for this book is available from the British Library.

Paperback ISBN: 9781036704476

The EU GPSR authorised representative is Logos Europe, 9 rue Nicolas Poussion, 17000 La Rochelle, France contact@logoseurope.eu

By M.J. Caan

The Shifter Wars

The Girl with the Good Magic
Enter the Wolf
The Return of the Witch

Paranormal Fades

Midlife Crashing
Midlife Burning
Midlife Rising

Midlife Enclave

Tantric Hexes
Tantric Bindings

Earth's First

Earth's First
Dark Days
A Hero Rises
Rise Of The Acolytes

Singing Falls Witches

Hex After Forty
That Good Hex
How Torie Got Her Hex Back
Hex and Chocolate
Moonlight Hexes
Hex and the Single Witch
Hex Education
Hex After Dark
That Hex Factor

For my one true Sorcerer Supreme, B

Chapter One

Sure, a forest can be romantic and beautiful... babbling brooks, dappled sunlight flowing through the leaves and all that. But on a night with no light from the moon, and clouds obscuring any stars above, it can also be creepy as fuck.

And creepy-ass woods might be the last place I wanted to be, but for right now it's exactly where I needed to be. I found a good-sized tree to hide behind, one that afforded me a clear view of the path ahead. It was big enough, however, to keep me shielded and out of sight for the moment. The good thing about the woods at night was that there is very little wind, so I didn't have to worry about my scent carrying and warning my prey of my presence.

At least I hoped that was the case. I hoped that I wasn't the prey. I shuddered, and pushed that thought the back of my head. First things first: I had to locate her. I reached down, grabbed my magic, and breathed out an augmentation spell. I focused the spell onto my eyes, and it allowed me to see clearly in the near-dark of the woods. As I peered out from behind the tree, everything around me took on an eerie glow. My vision range was shorter than what my human eyes would perceive in the daylight; about thirty paces ahead, everything faded into a blur. I concentrated again, this time shifting my vision to perceive the thermal range.

There! Twenty feet to my right I made out a red outline pressed against the cold darkness of the trees and leaves. The difference between the body temperature and the coolness of the canopy is unmistakable. Now all I had to do was figure out how to get the drop on her.

I concentrated and cast a shimmer over my body. I had to be careful; the normal blue hue of my magic would have stood out like a signal flare to her eyes. A shimmer was designed to mask one's physical presence as well as dampen sound. As long as it was active I would blend in seamlessly with the foliage around me, effectively making me invisible even to someone whose eyes were accustomed to the dark. I moved quickly across the open path, knowing that the shimmer should mask my sound, and wanting to end this as quickly as possible.

A few quick strides, and I was at her back. I grasped the hilt of the knife in my belt, drawing it and charging it with my magic, while in the same moment dropping the shimmer spell. Just as I raised the glowing blade overhead to start the downward plunge, she turned around and looked at me.

"Allie, wait! It's me!"

I halted the blade inches from Cody's face.

"Jesus! What the hell?" he said, looking up at me.

"I thought you were her!" I replied. "You're crouched down here by a tree and all I could make out was your heat signature. I thought you were trying to flush her out from the other side?"

"I was chasing her, I was right behind her and then... I lost her right in this area."

"What do you mean you lost her? You're a wolf! How can you lose anyone?" I was keeping my voice low and speaking only in hushed tones, although I was pretty sure our location was blown at this point.

A sudden rustling of leaves coming from above told us that she had gotten the drop on the two of us. I looked up just in time to see a black form dropping down from the canopy on top of us. I managed to get my shield up just as her roar filled the air. Sparks flew from my shield where her claws swiped at it. The impact shook me to my core but the shield held, and the heavy body bounced off into the undergrowth. Her massive body hit the ground and rolled, bringing her back to her feet. Almost instantly, a single bound took her up, over the shrubbery, and crashing through the woods once again.

"Now, Cody! Go!" I threw a ball of blue magic in the direction the panther had disappeared, lighting up the night sky and the surrounding terrain. Instantly, Cody shifted to his wolf-form and crashed after the Were-Panther with blinding speed. I followed behind, sprinting as hard as I could, but knowing I was no match for either of them in the speed department. A howl and a crash from ahead told me that Cody had either caught up with her or she had turned to confront him. Either way, I ignored the burning in my lungs and the cramping in my legs and pressed on until I reached a clearing—where the two Shifters appeared to be circling one another.

Despite the fact that in human-form Cody was much larger than Kendra, in their were-shapes they seemed to be equally sized. Just as I came into view, Kendra pounced on Cody. Her sleek panther form was nearly the same jet black as Cody's; the only difference was that her coat was shiny and short compared to the long, double layer of thick black hair that made up Cody's fur. Their large bodies crashed together as they rolled across the clearing, snapping dried logs and timber beneath them.

The collision of bodies brought them closer to me. Cody came up out of the roll and bolted to the side, a split-second before the panther could regain her footing. It was the only opening that I needed. I willed a bolt of magical force into my hand and hurled it at the Shifter. The blue blast hit her square in the side, driving her to the ground. The panther was clearly shaken; she was slow to get back up, and a low, threatening growl emanated from deep within her chest as she eyed me.

I watched as she gathered her powerful legs beneath her in preparation to spring—but that was when Cody struck. In the blink of an eye he had shifted from wolf-form to his hybrid shape. His body grew leaner. A light coat of black fur peppered his sinewy form. His face took on a slightly elongated look, his square jaw lengthening to make room for razor sharp fangs. His ears grew pointed and flattened against the side of his head. His eyes were almond-shaped and glowed bright yellow as he pounced on the Were-Panther, wrapping his powerful arms around her chest and lifting her into the air. The panther wasn't expecting such an attack, and all she could do was roar in displeasure, claws raking at the air, as she sought to twist her supple body free of his grasp.

"Now, Allie! Hurry!" Cody said.

I could tell from his strained tones he was having a hard time holding the Shifter. I lost no time in rushing up beside the struggling pair. I summoned my magic and thrust it into the were-panther, reaching deep beyond her conscious thought into that primal, bestial part of the brain that was beyond her control. There, I found the keys, the mystical pathway that controlled shifting I was looking for and began to play them in a sequence I had recently learned. The panther grew still, her roars subsiding, her flailing limbs going limp as she slowly began to shift, reverting back to her human form.

We released her as her transformation completed, dropping her to the ground. Cody shifted back into his human form as well, and stepped back to regard the both of us.

"Quicker than last time, but still you guys were way too clumsy," said Kendra. "I mean, I'm probably nowhere near as fast as a vampire, and I still didn't really have a hard time evading you."

I sighed and powered down, locking my magic away deep inside of me once again.

"She's right," said Cody. "We never even thought to look up in the trees. She got the drop on us like a couple of rank amateurs, which, if you think about it, is really what we are."

"I know, I know," I said. "But practice makes perfect. I mean, we did way better this time than the first time we tried this exercise."

"You almost stabbed me," said Cody.

I rolled my eyes at his exaggeration. "No way. Not even close to that." This elicited a laugh from Kendra. She looked from one of us to the other, her dark eyes sparkling in the night.

"Look," she started, "I'm willing to play these war games as long as you need. But in all honesty, I've rarely even met other Shifters. I've heard rumors of vampires existing, but neither me nor any other Shifter I've ever spoken to has ever actually met a vampire. If the rumors about them are true, you chasing me around the woods is not really going to prepare you for the real thing."

"See, that's just it," I said. "All we know are rumors. We have no idea what the real thing will be like."

"Well," said Cody, "we can pretty much agree that all rumors aside, vampires are the apex predators of supernaturals. They are strong and fast and effective killers."

"Exactly," I said, turning to Kendra, "and you're the closest thing we can find to that. As a panther, your strength and speed will hopefully imitate what we would be up against."

We were heading out of the woods led by the faint, blue glow of a magical sphere I had summoned. Unlike my two companions, I was incapable of seeing in the dark, and was grateful for the light. As we exited from under the dense trees into an opening, I turned to Kendra. "So, how are you finding things here in Trinity Cove?"

"I'm getting used to it," she replied after a pause. "It's not easy… I mean, it wasn't hard leaving my old life behind. That was a life of pain, and shame. But it was a pain that I knew; a pain I was familiar with. Starting over again here in this idyllic setting was scary. Sometimes the pain you know is more comforting than fear of the unknown."

Something in her tone told me that she wanted to say more, but I sensed that now was not the time.

A year ago, I destroyed the forbidding, an ancient spell created by my mother to contain rampant supernatural and magical energies, and in doing so saved Cody from a mystical poison. Ever since then, Shifters have been reappearing in the world—humans, many of whom had no idea they were Shifters until the whisper of magic touched them, and some who remembered what they were, but had been locked away from their abilities. Many of them made their way to Trinity Cove, the wellspring of the magic that had created them. Like many, Kendra had decided to settle in the woods around Singing Falls. The vast camp grounds were beginning to fill up with RVs where many Shifters were content to create their own little community away from the heart of the town. Eventually, they would probably move in closer, renting apartments, buying real estate, creating businesses, just like any residents moving into a new community. But the fact that they were Shifters, and were new to their abilities, made them wary of humans. It would take some time for them to adjust and trust their new neighbors.

As for the humans that lived in Trinity Cove, most were blissfully unaware of the changes taking place around them. There were some, mostly older, who had been in Trinity since before the Warlock I had mistakenly freed had attacked our community, and those residents recognized and welcomed the return of the supernaturals. Among those few there were a handful that reacted with fear. They remembered the days of the Warlocks and the werewolves hunting in their streets. Still, despite their unease, they welcomed the strangers into town.

Cody and I kept a low profile, taking in the new lay of the land. Cody's work as a deputy allowed him insight into sensitive situations before they became public knowledge. There were members of the police force that knew exactly what was going on; they knew who I was and who my family was. They didn't exactly turn a blind eye, but they trusted Cody when he volunteered to take point on anything that appeared to be of a more supernatural origin.

As for me, things were starting to look up. Business at

the coffee shop I ran had definitely picked up. I had developed a cast of regulars that came in after school or after work that I was beginning to get to know on a first-name basis. Most days between six and nine, the large mahogany leather club chairs arranged around coffee tables with gaming boards inlaid into their centers were all taken. Despite my aunts' initial disagreement about changes made to their store, my upgrades of installing WiFi, adding the new furniture, and offering free coffee refills had brought in patrons that quickly became regulars. Most of them were young, but there were quite a few of the older townsfolk that seemed to enjoy a nightly espresso while reading the local paper and pretending to be annoyed at all the chatter and clatter of laptops around them.

As for my aunts, they would occasionally swing through to see how things were going while squinting and making disapproving clicks with their tongues. But their disapproval quickly faded at the end of each week when I would show them the business tallies for the shop. Aunt Lena had even brought in batches of her homemade teabags to offer up for sale. Typically, they disappeared as soon as she dropped them on the counter, and while she might have acted annoyed, I could tell that she secretly loved the fact that her herbs were so desired.

I attributed the popularity of the coffee shop to free WiFi and refills. However, Cody had once told me that word had spread amongst certain members of the town community about how I had worked to restore the natural balance of magic in Trinity Cove. The fact that many of the new regulars frequenting my coffee shop had the unmistakable air of a Shifter about them attested to that fact. Whatever the reason, I was grateful not only for the increase in business, but for the fact that I didn't seem to be as much of a pariah as I had been before the fall of the Forbidding.

It was almost enough to make me forget that a crazed Warlock, in service to an ages-old vampire, was out to kill me. Almost.

Hence the late-night training exercises. Despite the trove of books in my aunts' library, there were no hardcore descriptions of true vampires and what they were capable of doing. If I was going to be in their crosshairs then I was going to be ready. And since I couldn't find a vampire to fight, a Were-Panther was the next best thing.

A sharp scream in the distance snapped me out of my reverie.

"The camp!" said Kendra.

In the blink of an eye, she shifted to her panther-form, and sprinted in the direction of the encampment she shared with other members of the Shifter community. Cody and I sprinted after her at a much slower pace, making our way through the brush until we reached the clearing at the edge of the woods. There, Kendra and other members of her community had set up RVs and makeshift tents.

Kendra, in human form, was standing next to an older woman who was wailing inconsolably.

"What is it? What happened?" I managed to ask between puffs of breath.

Kendra turned to face Cody and me. "Her grandson. She said her grandson was just taken."

"Taken?" said Cody. "Taken by whom?"

Kendra's eyes narrowed and flashed yellow as she stared at Cody.

"Taken by a wolf," she said. "She said that a wolf came into camp and carried her grandson off into the woods."

"Which way did they go?" I said.

By this time more people had gathered around us, having been awakened by the woman's screams. Everyone looked as she pointed to a break in the trees on the other side of the expanse.

Before I could say anything, Cody had shifted into his wolf-form and shot across the open space, heading into the woods.

"Stay here!" I said to Kendra as I turned and sprinted after Cody. I summoned my magic and willed it into my hands as I ducked into the tree-line, chasing two wolves and a stolen child.

Chapter Two

I crashed through the low-hanging branches, throwing blue-light magic ahead of me so I could see where I was going. I could hear Cody crashing through the underbrush, his lupine eyes not requiring magic to see. I muttered a useless curse at myself for not being able to keep up. I could only hope that if Cody found the Wolf he wouldn't engage until I was there. I stumbled out of the woods onto a small game path in the midst of the thickets. A few feet to my right, I could see Cody outlined in my flickering magic. He was sniffing at the game trail, trying to pick up the other Wolf's scent.

He growled before I could catch my breath or ask him which way to go. He looked to his left, and again took off following the trail. I ran after him, willing the burning ache in my lungs to dissipate. Just when I thought I couldn't run any longer I burst into a small, treeless patch of earth and almost tripped over Cody, who had stopped at the edge of the glen. His body was stiff, the dark hair along his back standing up as he growled, his gaze focused on something ahead. My eyes strained to pick up what he was seeing in the shadows.

"Fuck it," I said. I gathered a ball of magic in my hands and threw it into the air, where it split apart into a hundred sparkling shards that cascaded down like fireworks on the Fourth of July, illuminating everything around them. Suddenly the glen lit up as bright as day, and I could make out the form of a young boy lying on the ground.

I could also make out the form of a large gray wolf pacing back and forth around the boy. His tiny body wasn't moving, and even in the light of magic I couldn't tell if he was alive or dead. But then I heard it: a tiny whimper of fear escaped his little mouth.

The muscles in Cody's haunches flexed as he prepared to spring forward.

"No, wait!" I cried.

The gray wolf must have sensed Cody's intentions. It stopped pacing, and lowered its massive fangs to within inches of the boy's head. The warning growl told us that if either of us made a move, a quick snap would end the stolen child's life.

We were stuck. We didn't dare advance, and the wolf didn't bite. The stalemate did give me a chance to reach out with a slight tendril of magic. I could taste the wolf on the tip of my tongue, the sharp acrid bite of dark magic that surrounded it. There was no mistaking it; this was definitely a Shifter. Other than Cody and the one that had attacked us in Dr. Garner's house, there had been no sightings of wolf Shifters since I had destroyed the forbidding. As far as I knew, a wolf Shifter was always accompanied by one of the Order of the Fell, the mystical henchmen of the Warlock and the vampire Mallis. But no matter how deeply I probed into the surrounding woods, I could sense no other sign of magic. It was just the three of us and one whimpering child.

"Wait for my signal," I whispered to Cody. I spoke in a tone that was so quiet that I hoped even the supernatural hearing of a werewolf would not be able to pick it up. To his credit, Cody gave no indication that I said anything; his attention instead remained focused on the wolf that loomed ahead of us.

I began to lightly whisper a spell. My first instinct was to hurl a mystical hex bolt at the wolf and fry it before it could make a snack of the child. But something about its demeanor and the look in its eyes told me that that wasn't the best of ideas. No, this would call for subtlety, not a battering ram approach.

I concentrated on my magic, and breathed what I needed into existence. It was called ghosting, and it came from a set of glimmer magics that I had been practicing. I willed my magic to form a perfect three-dimensional image of myself that was indistinguishable from the real thing, even by another practitioner of magic. Once I was confident that the image was in place, I stepped back, the magic also shielding the physical me from perception.

I split my focus, using magic to maintain my illusion while also using it to dampen the sounds of my physical body as I circled around to flank the wolf. The closer I got to the Shifter, the more sick to my stomach I felt. Whatever magic had given rise to this being was so dark and powerful that I felt like I was being smothered. I was close enough that I could feel the heat being radiated by the wolf's body. I watched in revulsion as the creature lowered its head enough that its flickering tongue grazed the top of the boy's head.

It was tasting the child. My stomach turned as I sensed

the hunger and desire inside of the beast. Enough of this bullshit. I dropped the cloak of magic that shielded me from the wolf's senses, and channeled it into my hands in a ball of raw power.

I struck with all the fury I could muster, aiming a blast of power at the creature's side. I was surprised at the speed with which the wolf reacted: despite my cloaking, as soon as I dropped my spell to go on the offensive the wolf sensed my presence.

It turned with blinding speed, a mass of gray tooth and claw hurling at me before I could unleash my power. In a flash, the beast was on top of me. I felt like I was being crushed beneath its massive weight as it snarled and snapped for my throat. I managed to get my forearm up in front of my face, stifling a panicked scream. I felt three-inch-long canines bite through my leather coat and deep into the muscle of my arm. The pain sent shockwaves through my body and my magic flared out reflexively. Blue power lashed at the wolf, throwing it off of my chest.

The wolf was thrown backward and hit the forest floor with a heavy grunt. I ignored the searing pain that ripped through my forearm. Instead, I channeled the adrenaline rush into my magic, and cast a shimmering protective field around myself and the child, cowering on the ground beside me. I reached down to place a comforting hand on the poor boy's head, trying to calm him even as I felt the immense weight of the Shifter crashing into my force field. I looked up in time to see the gray wolf take a couple of steps back and then charge forward, slamming its full weight into my shield. My whole body shook with the impact, but one of the things I had been practicing was maintaining protective barriers. No way was I letting this beast get to myself or that little boy.

Just as I was about to draw up more magic to lash out at the beast, a dark shape slammed into the wolf, sending it sprawling away from me. Cody took a second to give me a quick look before hurling his wolven form at the other Shifter. In the blink of an eye he advanced on the gray wolf, and used his bulk and muscle to pin it down before lunging out with his own considerable fangs, aimed at the soft underside of the beast's neck.

But before they could make contact with the vulnerable spot, the gray wolf shifted. In the blink of an eye the wolf assumed a hybrid form, lean, muscular and covered in velvety gray fur with humanoid features that mimicked Cody's when he was in that form. The new shape allowed it to twist out of what would have surely been a death blow. Cody's jaws snapped shut mere inches from the creature's carotid arteries. In hybrid form, the Shifter nimbly rolled out from under Cody, grasping tightly at the fur and skin of Cody's back with a clawed hand. With a powerful heave, the hybrid tossed Cody's massive form like it was nothing, out of the clearing and into the trees beyond.

Almost quicker than I could follow, the hybrid lunged at me, raking razor-sharp claws across the protective blue barrier that kept myself and my young charge alive. Sparks flew from my shield as the creature rained blow after blow onto it. Just when I thought I might not be able to maintain the barrier much longer, the beast stopped and stood back. That was when I got a good look at it.

Except the creature wasn't an "it" at all; it was most definitely a "she".

In hybrid form I could definitely make out the curves, lithe musculature, and breasts of a female figure. Gray fur covered her from head to toe and sparkled in the eerie luminescence of my magic. She stepped back and leered at us, her lips drawing back from impossibly long fangs. Maybe it was the stress of the situation, but I could have sworn that she smiled at me before turning and leaping into the air, her form twisting, transforming back into a full wolf to land on all fours and sprint off into the woods.

I dropped my magic just as Cody came sprinting up. He shifted back to full human-form and stood beside me, just as I was helping the small boy to his feet.

"What happened?" he asked. "Where's the werewolf?"

"I don't know; she just ran off into the woods," I answered.

"She?"

I nodded without saying anything as I looked down at the small child beside us. He didn't seem to be any worse for wear, I decided, examining the puncture marks in the back of his shirt where the wolf had dragged him. Before I could say anything, Cody spun away from us, looking off into the distance.

"What is it?" I said. I could sense Cody drawing on his Shifting abilities, his head tilted to one side as he processed something I could not hear. Whatever it was, it was enough to spring his claws free. That, and the tension in his body, caused me to draw up a flame of blue magic and hold it in my hands.

"Screams," he said, turning to face me, "and… gunfire!"

Suddenly, I realized why the wolf had cut her attack short.

"The encampment!" I said. "This attack was just a ploy to draw us away from the Shifter camp."

Cody snatched up the young child, and I followed him, running as quickly as I could, as we headed back toward the encampment.

Chapter Three

As we got closer to the encampment, I could make out the cries and wails of fear and pain. The acrid stench of smoke hit me as we broke from the last bit of trees and undergrowth right before the clearing.

I was breathing hard, and sucking lungfuls of smoke was causing me to cough almost uncontrollably. The smoke stung my eyes; through the tears I could make out that a few of the tents that had been pitched near the RVs were on fire. The RVs had been the target of the fires, but the sparks from the campers had also landed on top of a few of the tents, setting them ablaze.

Chaos had set in. Many in the Shifter community were running to and fro, some of them carrying small children to safety while others battled the fires with portable extinguishers. Immediately, I was filled with fear, as every movie containing a scene with a burning vehicle played out in my mind. I wasn't sure if cars really burst into giant fireballs after burning for a few minutes, or if that was just a Hollywood effect that was created by one enterprising director, and had since spread to every movie ever shot containing a blazing vehicle. But then I remembered that most RVs contain propane gas tanks of some kind—either as a heat source or cooking source—and that even if the gasoline tanks didn't erupt, those most definitely would.

Three RVs were burning, their flames transitioning from bright orange to white against the black sky. I sprinted toward them, unsure of my exact plan. If they did blow, they would take out a sizable chunk of this camp, and who knows how many of the innocent Shifters would also fall.

I stood as close as I could to the inferno, then closed my eyes and spread my arms wide. I had gotten pretty good at starting fires, but I had never really considered the mechanics of putting one out. Especially not one that had not been created by, or as a response to, my magic. While that thought was frightening, it also gave me an idea. I concentrated, and willed my own magic to pour into the flames. Instantly, I almost regretted it; whatever my magic touched, I touched, and vice versa. I stifled a scream as I was hit with the sensation that every inch of my flesh was suddenly being seared.

Instead I blocked out the massive rush of heat and concentrated on the task at hand. I felt my magic begin to infuse the flames, taking over their warmth and turning them from white-hot to cool blue. However, the effort of corralling the flames was taking its toll. I could feel my teeth grinding together so hard that I was sure they would shatter in my mouth. Every fiber of my being cried out for me to stop, but I was way too stubborn to give in to voices in my head. Just when I thought I couldn't expend any more energy, I started to call my magic back. I could feel it retreating within me, and with it the angry flames that were threatening to destroy the camp.

It felt like my skin was splitting open. Slowly I drew my power, and with it the fire, back into my body. I still didn't open my eyes, but I knew the danger was gone; I could feel the change in the temperature around me. The cool, crisp mountain air had returned, and the acrid smoke no longer clawed at my nostrils. I suddenly felt like a puppet with cut strings as I dropped to my hands and knees, weakened beyond the telling. I began to cough uncontrollably, each forceful exhalation expelling black smoke out of my lungs and onto the ground in front of me.

"Hey, easy there," said Cody. He was standing next to me and had bent over to place a reassuring hand on my back. "You okay?"

"Yeah, I think so," I replied. The coughing and the smoke coming out of me had finally subsided, and I was able to regain my footing.

"Okay, that was impressive," Cody said as he continued to massage my back. "And you are burning up!" He raised one hand and placed it against my face. It felt like I was being touched by a soft, smooth blanket of ice.

"Better me than all of them," I said, nodding at the Shifters that were starting to gather around us. I noticed that the small fires that were threatening the tents had been put out, and most of the inhabitants' attention seem to be focused on me and Cody. "Is everyone okay? What happened?"

I looked around, but all I could make out was confusion and fear on the faces that had gathered to gawk at us.

"They made good on their threat." It was the old woman who spoke up—the one whose young charge was taken by the wolf. She now clutched the young boy fiercely to her side, her tattered old shawl draped protectively around his shoulders, his face buried deeply into her neck.

"What threats? And who made them?" I asked.

The assembly that circled us murmured amongst themselves, but no one spoke up.

Finally, the old woman stepped forward. "Those cult members, or whatever they are, that have been coming around here lately...they're looking for witches and Shifters that are willing to join up with them." She spat onto the ground beside her and stared at me, her eyes narrowed and filled with fury and hatred, but at what, I couldn't tell. "They said that any Shifters that remained here would be sorry. They said a war was coming and anybody who wasn't with them would be treated like an enemy. They suggested that we all leave and go back to where we came from."

"These cult members," Cody said, "were they all dressed in black?"

"Well of course they were," said the old woman. "I told you, they're cult members; what else do they wear?" I would have laughed, except the anger in her voice told me that she wasn't trying to be funny.

"So they did this?" I asked. "They set fire to your camp to try to scare you away?"

"How long is this been going on?" Cody said.

"About a week now," she replied. "They first showed up and started offering fistfuls of money to Shifters who would join their cause. When they didn't get many of us to jump at the offer, they started making threats. Told us we would regret this. I guess now we know they were serious."

"I guess this confirms what we were thinking; the wolf that stole the child was a distraction," I said, turning to Cody. "That was just meant to draw the two of us away from the camp so that whoever was working with the wolf could do this. Thank God no one was hurt seriously."

"Well, hopefully not too seriously." The voice floated

from the back of the assembled Shifters. It sounded weak and filled with pain. Before anyone could reply, a small figure cut its way through the crowd to approach me and Cody.

It was Kendra, her gait unsteady and her head hanging down. Both of her arms were clutched around her waist as she stumbled forward on legs that looked like they could barely support her weight.

"But this—" she held up one shaky hand that was covered something wet and thick "—kind of feels pretty serious."

Cody managed to catch her just as she tumbled forward, lapsing into unconsciousness. She was covered in blood from a wound in her abdomen.

"My God!" said Cody. "She's been shot!" He lifted her into his arms to cradle her frighteningly still figure.

"Somebody get a blanket!" I said, rushing to his side. Her still figure seemed tiny and fragile in his arms.

"We need to get her to a hospital," Cody said as a member of the community ran forward to drape an old, checkered blanket over her.

I placed two fingers on her neck, feeling for a pulse. It was slow and weak, but there nonetheless. The blanket that covered her was already beginning to show a dark spot where it made contact with her torn flesh.

I looked up at Cody and shook my head. "We can't take her to a hospital; it would raise too many questions—the kind of questions that even you won't be able to bury."

"We can't just let her die!" Cody said.

"We're not going to," I said, looking up at him. "She doesn't need a hospital, but she does need a doctor."

Chapter Four

Even though I understood why Cody was reluctant to call for a police escort, I found myself wishing he would—if for no other reason than to have the few cars that were out in the middle of the night pull aside for us. Instead, he drove like a maniac, weaving around traffic as we sped from the Falls into town. I rode in the back of his car with Kendra's head cradled in my lap. The only piece of clean cloth we could find was one of Cody's spare deputy uniform tops. I kept that pressed to the wound in Kendra's abdomen, trying desperately to staunch the flow of blood.

I had tried to help her with magic, but every time I probed her she seemed to be hit with new spasms of pain. The truth of the matter was that I had very little knowledge of human anatomy. I wasn't skilled enough in the use of magic to help her, and for all I know I was doing more damage than good.

"Hurry, Cody! How much farther?"

"We're almost there," he said without taking his eyes off the road. "Just keep pressure on that wound."

The blood had nearly soaked the shirt, and I couldn't help but notice that Kendra's skin had grown cold and clammy. Her dark hair was wet with sweat and clung to her face. I looked up, scanning the surroundings as they flashed by.

Thank God, I thought, as we flashed by the coffee shop. Not far now.

"Hold on, Kendra. Just a little longer," I whispered to her.

Cody took a quick right off of Main Street, and pulled into the driveway of a large Victorian. It was one of many that lined the small back streets that ran behind the commercial district of Trinity Cove. The houses were set up with dual permits, many housing businesses on the first floor and then living quarters for the owners of the second floor.

Tires squealed as Cody slammed on the brakes. The car had barely settled when he was already out of it and rushing around to open the back passenger door. He carefully scooped up Kendra into his arms while I ran to the front door of the house, to slam my palm repeatedly against it while ringing the doorbell simultaneously.

In what felt like hours, but in reality was probably less than a minute, the door swung open, and I was face to face with Isla Garner.

"Allie? Girl, what in the..." Her voice trailed off as I stepped aside and Cody rushed past me with Kendra cradled in his arms.

The entryway of the Victorian led into a small reception area that had been set up to receive and register patients. Beyond that, there was a doorway that led to a couple of exam rooms, just before opening onto what used to be a sunporch, but had now been enclosed and fitted with a variety of small kennels, most of which were empty.

A chorus of barks greeted us as Cody burst through the room and entered one of the smaller exam bays. He gently placed Kendra onto one of the tables.

"Officer Hunter," Isla said, "who is this girl? What going on?" Even though it was the middle of the night, her adrenaline seemed to be kicking in and any traces of sleep and confusion had quickly vanished.

"She's a friend," Cody said, "and she's been shot."

"You have to help her," I pleaded.

The look of shock on the veterinarian's face as she looked from Kendra to me, and then to Cody, scared me. It made me question my decision to bring Kendra to her.

"Why the hell is she here?" said Dr. Garner. "She needs to be in a hospital."

I exchanged looks with Cody, and he nodded.

"Isla... Dr. Garner," I began, "we can't take her to a hospital because she's... different."

She just stared at me, silently weighing her options. Then she rushed around to the side of the table where Kendra lay and motioned for Cody to help her. Together, the two of them carefully rolled Kendra up onto her side, away from Dr. Garner.

"What are you doing?" I asked as Dr. Garner bent to examine Kendra.

"I'm looking for an exit wound, since it's pretty obvious she's been shot." She felt around for a few seconds before looking up at me. "There isn't one; that means the bullet is still inside of her. That's the first order of business, digging it out." They rolled Kendra back into a supine position on the table. The motion elicited a sharp gasp of pain as her eyes fluttered open.

She moaned and coughed as spasms racked her body. I

moved to her side and took her hand, bending down to speak in her ear.

"Easy there," I said. "You're with a friend, and she's going to help you. Just try to relax."

"Allie," she gasped, squeezing my hand.

"I'm here, Kendra, but don't try to talk; just relax and let the doctor help you," I replied, pushing a clinging strand of black hair away from her face.

"No, I need to... I have to get back... You don't understand," she pleaded. "I remember what they said when they shot me. It's Mallis. He intends to bring about the Leveling. You have to... You have to stop him."

Before I could say anything, another spasm of pain caused her body to twist uncontrollably, and was accompanied by a terrifying scream through clenched teeth.

"Hey!" shouted Dr. Garner. "No more talking! If I'm going to save her, I need her still and cooperative."

Cody and I were struggling to hold her still on the table just as the door to the exam room burst open. I looked up as a lithe female figure rushed into the room. She was on the shorter side, standing at about five feet two. She had olive-toned skin, and jet-black hair with a striking purple streak, pulled up in a high ponytail. She was barefoot, and dressed in a pair of boy shorts and a black T-shirt with a picture of Darth Vader on it, emblazoned with the word #RESIST in orange letters. But what really caught my eye was the weapon she brandished in her right hand.

She brandished a thin, silver rapier, roughly three feet in length, barely half an inch at the base and tapering to an impossibly sharp point at the end. An intricately carved silver hilt curved downward to protect the fencer's hand that gripped the weapon. The woman herself resembled the blade: lean, flexible, and fluid— she had slid into the room like a trained dancer. No, not a dancer; a fighter. Judging by the way she held the blade, probably a fencer.

"Esmay, no!" said Dr. Garner. "These are friends, and they've brought a patient that needs immediate attention."

As soon as she said her name, I recognized the young woman as the office receptionist. She had often come into my shop during the middle of the day to purchase two double shot espressos. She was always dressed in an immaculate pantsuit and heels that gave her an illusion of height that made her look like an entirely different person. However, she also wore an office name tag, and I remember commenting on her name. Esmay. But what was she doing here in the middle of the night?

"Babe, please, I promise you everything is okay. I just need you to run into the other room and get me the gray surgical kit that's locked in the cabinet—the one I use for very special occasions." She gave Esmay a pointed look and the young woman nodded before running out of the room.

"Babe", huh? Well, that answered my question.

"I can't triage her like this," Dr. Garner said. She gave me a long look before continuing. "I need her to Shift into...whatever animal form she takes." The fact that I returned her stare only seemed to make her more angry. "Look," she continued, "I'm a veterinarian. I treat animals, not humans. If you want me to have the best chance at saving your friend, she needs to...not be human. Besides, her animal form is a lot stronger than this one. It will give her the best chance of survival."

I nodded and leaned over, placing my mouth close to Kendra's ear. "Kendra. Kendra, can you hear me? I need you to Shift for me; can you do that?"

It was no use; she had lapsed into unconsciousness once

again. Barely audible, shallow breaths escaped her slightly parted lips.

"Allie, do it," said Cody. "Force her to Shift."

"What if it kills her?" I said, looking up.

"Well, if she stays like this she's probably going to die anyway," said Dr. Garner. "Whatever you're going to do, you'd better do it now."

I took Kendra's head in both of my hands and closed my eyes just as Esmay reentered the room. She carried a gray briefcase around the table to Dr. Garner. I willed my magic to flow into Kendra until I sensed the same primal spark that flows within all Shifters. I reached for that spark and gathered it within the blue light of my magic. I breathed life into it, commanding it to grow into a raging inferno. My eyes were clear and focused when I looked at the young woman dying on the table in front of me, and spoke a single word.

"Shift."

In an instant her slender form was gone, replaced by the majestic, massive form of a Were-Panther. Briefly, a pair of green eyes looked up at me before once again closing, the massive furred head I was now holding once again slumped against the table. At least she was still breathing, but the low, raspy sound of the creature's breath did little to reassure me that Kendra was going to live through this night.

"Whoa," said Esmay, "I've never seen one in person like this." She reached out one tentative hand and ran her fingers through Kendra's sable-like fur.

"All right then," said Dr. Garner as she sprang into action. "Esmay, get her on the monitor, draw some blood, and go match it quickly. I have a feeling she's going to need a lot of it to pull through this. You two—go and have a seat in the waiting room. I'll be out as soon as I have some news."

She didn't even look at us as she gave her commands, but was instead lost in the contents of the gray case that Esmay had brought her. I was reluctant to leave, but I felt Cody's hand close over mine and he lightly tugged me toward the door.

We entered the waiting room, and my eye was immediately drawn to the Keurig machine that was set up on a small receiving table at the far end of the space. I made my way over to it and began to peruse the various flavors on display. I felt Cody walk up behind me and envelop me in his strong arms, pulling me close. He kissed me lightly on the top of the head before resting his cheek against mine.

"Are you okay?" he asked.

I turned my body in his arms so that I could look him eye to eye, and then buried my face in the comfort of his strong chest. He still smelled like smoke, but that didn't bother me; I took comfort in his very presence.

"Did you know?" I asked.

"About?"

"About the threats made to the encampments."

His silence told me what I needed to know.

"I only became aware of the threats the last few weeks. The Shifters came to me because they knew what I was. I promised I would keep it quiet as I looked into things."

I turned, shaking my head, as I picked out a mahogany roast K-cup. "But why keep it from me?"

"Because after everything that you've been through, I thought this was the last thing that you needed on your plate. Besides, things have been so quiet lately, I was hoping the town was finally getting back to normal."

"There's nothing normal about this town. There never

has been, and I'm starting to think there never will be. What happened up there, what happened to Kendra, is all my fault."

I felt his hands resting on my shoulders reassuringly just as the brewer finished filling my cup of coffee. I raised the steaming cup to my lips and took a tentative sip. Ugg, tasted like shit. Why do people still drink this mess?

"And that's why I didn't want to say anything," he said. "I knew you would just beat yourself up about this."

Despite the much-needed caffeine fix, I couldn't take any more of this swill in my cup. I set it down as I turned to face Cody. "But it is my fault. Despite all the warnings, I was the one that broke the forbidding. I dropped that veil and that's what freed the Warlock and has allowed all of this horror to exist again."

"If you hadn't done what you did, more likely than not I wouldn't be here now. So if you want to go down that road, then I'm as guilty as you in all of this. We can't go back and change the past, so we might as well focus on what's coming."

He was right, of course; crying over spilt milk was never for me. "I guess I just allowed myself to be hopeful that maybe the Warlock would have just moved on and set up shop somewhere else." I felt guilty for saying that; it was like I had let the cat out of the bag, and then stood aside and ignored it as it turned feral and began gobbling up all the other creatures around it.

"I think it's pretty clear that's not going to happen," said Cody. "I think he's hiding in the shadows, waiting to see what would happen as the magic began to flow through the ley lines once again. We were told he was building an army. He's been waiting for Shifters to return to this area so he could begin building the foundation for whatever plans his master Mallis has in mind."

I turned away from him and walked over to one of the chairs arranged against the wall, facing a desk. "Yes. Whatever this leveling is, we need to be prepared. But what do we do about protecting the Shifter community?"

"I don't think we have to worry as much about them. I mean, think about it. The Warlock has already gotten what he wants from that community: recruits for his army. The ones who stayed behind are ones who were not going to join him."

"If that's the case, why burn the camp? For that matter, why shoot Kendra?"

"I've been thinking about that. I think the fire was meant to distract us. Or to test us maybe, to see what we would do, how we would react. As for Kendra, she's a Were-Panther. That's a very powerful Shifter, and if she refused to join his little brigade…"

"It would be better to take her off the playing field than potentially have to face her in battle down the road," I finished.

"Exactly. And think about it: where were all the men at this encampment? The majority of the people there were either the elderly or the very young."

I nodded as the realization began to dawn on me. "So who knows how many recruits the Warlock has already made."

"But it's not just Shifters," said Cody. "He's also after witches."

"Yes, but those would be even harder to come by than Shifters right now. I mean, I would know if there were other witches in Trinity Cove. Wouldn't I?" Surely my aunts would've told me if there were new witches in the area.

"Who knows?" Cody continued. "With all the changes around here, is it so hard to believe that a witch could sneak into the area? There are all kinds of supernatural beings moving back to town. We have no idea what could be out there."

"Like that wolf, you mean?" He only nodded his head, and I had a feeling we were finally discussing what had been on his mind ever since we had left the camp.

"Allie, the way she moved, the raw power...it was unreal."

I knew what he meant. This Shifter was different from any we had faced so far.

"And how was she able to Shift into her hybrid form like that?" Cody continued. "It is your magic that has allowed me to control my Shifting to that degree."

"Also, up until now every Wolf we have encountered has had a member of the Fell close by, pulling its strings. I assumed that without one of them, the wolf could not Shift."

"Unless the Warlock has found a way to turn their Shifting abilities on, and give them complete control over them. Your magic did that for me; who's to say his magic can't do the same thing for them?"

"Which could help explain why they're looking for witches. The Warlock has no magic of his own; he can only siphon and use power from a true witch. Maybe he's looking for new batteries." Even as I said it, I cringed, hating the way it sounded. "And if that Wolf is any indication of what he's capable of creating, then we need to stop him before this goes any further."

"It may be more dangerous than you're thinking," said the voice of Dr. Garner as she entered the room. The smock she wore was splattered with blood, and in one latex gloved hand she carried a silver, kidney-shaped basin. She stretched out her arm for Cody and I saw what the bowl contained.

"Is that the bullet?" said Cody.

Dr. Garner nodded. "Yes it is. I was able to extract it; your friend should be fine. Shifters heal at a remarkably fast rate. But what you need to see is what this bullet is made of."

Cody reached into the pan and picked up the gleaming projectile. Instantly, he dropped it back into the basin with a clang, shaking his hand.

"Jesus," he said, opening and closing his hand as if to ward off the pins and needles of numbness. "Is that silver?"

Dr. Garner nodded. "Yes it is. And judging from the speed with which it was breaking down the tissue and muscle inside your friend, I would say it's pure silver—probably laced with a type of poison that only has a single purpose."

I stared at the bullet and then looked at Cody.

"It's to kill Shifters. More specifically, it's designed to kill werewolves," Dr. Garner said.

I swallowed hard, a chill creeping up my spine. This attack had not been a distraction or a test. It was a warning. Someone out there knew what Cody was. And they were sending us a very deadly message.

Chapter Five

I caught myself falling asleep multiple times on the ride back to the house. Cody didn't seem to mind, as we were both too exhausted to even make small talk. I couldn't remember ever being so happy to see my aunts' large Victorian at the top of the ridge overlooking the rest of Trinity Cove as I was this night.

A quick tap of the wards I had placed around the home let me know that nothing had been disturbed and no one had approached the house while we were out. My brother Gar was staying over at a friend's place, and without my aunts being home, the emptiness of the large house was a welcome respite after everything we had just been through. I felt the urge to call Gar to make sure that he was okay, but all that would accomplish would be eliciting a thousand questions and possibly scare him for no reason.

I tossed the keys into the bowl that sat on the small display table just inside the entryway. I turned to Cody and practically collapsed in his strong arms. I took his hand in mine and led him to my bedroom at the far end of the house. I wanted to collapse onto the bed, clothes and all, but before I could, Cody pulled me into the bathroom and began running the shower. I groaned, but realized it was needed. We both smelled like smoke, sweat and God knows what else.

We peeled off our clothes and left them in a single pile on the bathroom floor. The temperature of the water, along with the steam that the shower was generating, was an instant soothing balm to my skin. The water cascaded over both of us as Cody stood close behind me, his strong hands massaging a million tiny knots from my shoulders. I let my head fall back against his broad chest as my body relaxed.

He reached around me and removed one of my shampoo bottles from the built-in shelf. I became aware of tiny moans escaping my lips as he began to lather my hair, his fingers massaging my scalp gently. Despite the lethargy that crept into every muscle of my being, I felt heat beginning to stir deep inside me. And judging from the pressure that was suddenly pulsing against my lower back, I knew Cody felt it too.

Our longing only increased as Cody rinsed the shampoo from my hair, then lowered his lips to the side of my neck, one arm encircling my waist to pull me back against him. I gasped at the sensation before turning to press my body tightly against his. His kisses engulfed me, his breath coming in short gasps, as I slid my hand down his soapy abs to grasp a handful of flesh that was hotter than the water splashing down on us. We both smiled as we gave into our bodies, letting the tempo of our flesh burn away something that the cleansing shower could not.

Ignoring the fatigue, I rose early the next morning. Maybe I had been dreaming, or maybe my subconscious had been working out problems during my sleep. Either way, I had the beginnings of an idea formulating in the far banks of my mind as I slipped into a T-shirt and a pair of sweatpants and padded quietly into my aunts' office.

While it was still off limits to Gar, my aunts no longer forbade me to enter. They knew I had been studying the vast amounts of knowledge collected in the volumes of leather-bound tomes that lined the floor-to-ceiling bookcases. I had come to understand that most of the arcane knowledge contained in these books might have been beyond my aunts' abilities—or willingness—to utilize. But that was not the case with me. I was a Reliquary, so in theory my innate ability to work magic had should not have hit any limitations. But as I found out with my inability to heal Kendra, that may not have be true in my case.

A simple seeking spell helped me locate the book that I needed. I flipped through the pages until I found what I was looking for, and quickly memorized the ritual. I slid the book back on the shelf and exited the office, nearly bumping into Cody on his way to the stairs that led us to the main level of the house.

"Anything interesting?" he asked, after giving me a quick peck on the forehead.

"Actually, I did have an idea. There's something I want to try that I think will help us in this situation. But...after breakfast; I'm starving."

I led Cody to the large kitchen that dominated the main floor of the house. A quick perusal of the refrigerator revealed Canadian bacon, eggs, sausage, some feta cheese, and spinach, as well as some orange juice from the day before—everything I needed to make a hearty frittata. I set about prepping the breakfast, and tasked Cody with preparing the coffee.

I felt the cool blast of morning air as Cody opened the French doors that led from the kitchen onto the deck. As the eggs settled in the skillet, I went to grab a sweater from the front closet before joining Cody on the deck. He was on his cell phone, and I could make out the words "thank you" as he hung up, just as I reached the side.

He turned to me and smiled. "That was Dr. Garner. She said Kendra is doing fine, although she needs to keep her at the clinic for another couple of days just to make sure she's completely out of the woods, and no infection sets in."

I close my eyes and breathed a sigh of relief. "Is she conscious? Can we talk to her?"

"No, not yet. But Dr. Garner did say she would call as soon as she wakes up."

I nodded and turned to go back into the house. This was good news, and already I could feel my spirits lifting. The frittata was nicely set and the smell of coffee wafting through the air only served to buoy my feelings even more. Cody went about filling two mugs with the rich brew and took them outside to the table. I divided the eggs, added a few pieces of fruit as sides, and placed both dishes onto a serving tray along with the orange juice.

The morning sun had yet to fully crest over the tree line to dry the dew that had settled on the cushions and the table surface. I reached into a brown rattan trunk that sat to one side of the deck, where my aunts kept extra cushions and blankets. I removed two large beach towels and placed them over the chairs before sitting down to breakfast.

"Well, so much for a simple training exercise," I said.

"She's going to be fine," replied Cody.

"It's not just her. It's the Shifters at the camp. It's Gar. My best friend, Hope. Hell, even you. I feel like I've brought so much darkness and danger into this town and to everyone I care for." I push my plate away, my appetite suddenly faded. "I mean, I didn't go looking for any of this."

"No, but maybe it found you for a reason. You know, maybe you're like...what's her name. That girl who had to kill all the vampires on that show everyone watched while we were in high school."

"Buffy?"

"Yes, that's the one! Maybe you're like the Chosen One and you have to be this town's protector."

I couldn't help but laugh. "You do know that no matter what genre, anybody who's ever 'the Chosen One' ends up dying."

"Well, on TV maybe, but this is real life, and you're not dying anytime soon." He winked, blew me a kiss, and reached across the table to give my hand a squeeze. "Now, what's this idea that you had?"

"Come on," I said, beginning to clear the table. "Do you have a map of the area in your car?" A quick nod confirmed that he did. Why anyone kept a map in this day and age, I had no idea, but for once I was thankful for old-fashioned printed paper. "Good. Grab it, meet me downstairs, and I'll show you."

After cleaning off the table and loading the dishwasher, I headed down to the lowest level of the house. The stairs ended in a generous hallway, with laundry and storage rooms flanking either side. It opened into a single cavernous room with double doors leading out to a lower deck. This was where Gar spent most of his time, sprawled on the couch playing video games on the big-screen TV. There were a couple of gaming tables and large reclining chairs off to one side as well.

Cody was already there, standing in front of the doors that led outside. "Okay, I got the map; where do you want it?"

"Over here," I replied, motioning to the large gaming table. "Spread it out so that we can see the entire thing."

The map had been folded accordion style, and when he opened it completely I was pleasantly surprised to see the entire town and surrounding areas clearly marked out.

"Now what?" he asked.

"Just watch." I reached into my pocket and withdrew a small Ziploc sandwich bag. Inside, I had poured a small bit of rock salt. I reached into the bag, gathered a large pinch of the salt, and held it high over the map. I opened my fingers and let it drop, scattering it all across the crisscrossing lines that represented Trinity Cove.

"And now, with just a little bit of magic…" I said. Then I concentrated, focusing my will on the desired outcome, and recited the incantation I had memorized. Instantly, the salt pebbles began to glow a soft blue, and swirled about across the surface of the map as if they were caught up in a miniature dust devil sweeping across the table. I opened my eyes, aware of the blue haze of magic that shone through them. "And now, reveal to me that which is hidden."

The salt pebbles immediately began to swirl faster, before coming together to form a single spinning ball. There was a slight pop as the ball split into individual grains of glowing blue pellets. Each pellet flew to a different area on the map and stuck in place. Then the entire room flashed blue, and something that sounded like thunder rumbled through the basement. Cody and I both shielded our eyes from the unexpected glare. Just as quickly as it appeared, the light faded, and we could once again focus on the map. But now there were tiny burns spots decorating the topography.

"What the hell was that?" said Cody.

I smiled as I realized my spell had worked. "That was a spell of revelation. All of these spots on the map represent supernaturals, including witches, Shifters and whatever else may have come to town recently."

Cody leaned over the table, studying the map. He frowned as he traced his fingers over the pockmarked paper. His hands stopped in one particular area where there was a larger concentration of tiny burn marks.

"And with this we are going to…what?" he said.

I looked up at him and gave him a wink. "Do you see the variances in the cluster groupings? Most of the markings are single pockmarks on the map. Witches don't usually live in groups together. We know the Shifter community is pretty much here," I said, pointing to the area on the map near Singing Falls that showed a cluster of supernatural activity, "but that still leaves a few more clusters dotting around the outskirts of town that are unaccounted for. They are either more bands of Shifters, or…"

"Or that's where the Warlock and his merry band of monsters is holding up! Brilliant! That puts us one step ahead of them!"

He was half right. I didn't have the heart to tell him the whole plan.

"So now it's your turn to work your cop magic," I said.

"What do you mean?" he asked.

"There are still a lot of hotspots showing. Isn't there some way you can use the tools at your disposal as Town Deputy to figure out which one of the supernaturals doesn't seem to gel with the law-abiding property owners? There has to be a way to at least narrow them down to who we are looking for, right?"

He thought about it for a minute before nodding his head. "You know, I think I might know just the thing we need."

Since the map was too big to adequately copy, I gave him the original just as he was about to leave the house. He kissed me at the door, long and slow.

"I'll call you later. Check in with me if you leave the house."

I rolled my eyes. "Jesus, now you sound like Aunt Vivian. But I promise to check in. I'm going to clean up here before Gar gets back, and then maybe swing by the clinic to see how Kendra is doing. I'm going to whip up some desserts to take to Dr. Garner to show our appreciation for everything she did."

"Okay," he replied. "Just be careful." He paused as he stepped outside the door. "And I will still be worried. So please answer when I text you."

I smiled and gave him an exaggerated look of annoyance before closing the door after him. I went back into the kitchen and looked up a recipe for cheesecake. Nearly everyone likes cheesecake, and I hoped that Isla Garner was no exception to that rule. Plus, it would help me keep my mind off what I had planned for later.

All I needed was the address where the Warlock was. Then it would be game on.

Chapter Six

Few things make me as happy as baking. It'd taken no time to whip up a graham cracker crust mixed with crushed Oreos, which I pressed into the bottom of my springform pan, then covered with a creamy, velvety New York style cheesecake. I placed it in the oven to bake and then set about creating a rich raspberry cream sauce that I would drizzle over the top of my creation. The smell throughout the house was decadent, and for a moment I wished I had made two; cheesecake was one of Gar's all-time favorite desserts.

Thinking of my brother caused me to make a mental note to text him before I headed over to Dr. Garner's. Not that I was worried, exactly, but he had been a little more withdrawn and quiet lately. I was sure it was just one of those mood swings that most teenagers go through. God knows I had been there—and then some. It's a wonder I made it out of my teenage years without one of my aunts turning me into a frog, or something else more manageable than a sixteen-year-old.

I checked on the raspberry topping that had been simmering away, and was just about to taste it when I felt a familiar brush against the wards around the house. I placed the wooden spoon I had been stirring with carefully on the saucer next to the stove, wiped my hands, and made my way to the door. I opened it just as Hope was reaching for the doorbell.

"Hey, girl, come on in," I said, turning to head back into the kitchen.

"Uh-uh, no," she said, closing the door and following me. "You do not get to 'hey, girl' me."

I had known this was coming and had dreaded it. I returned to the stove and slowly stirred the raspberry reduction.

"Where have you been?" Hope asked. "I have not heard from you in a couple of weeks now. I was imagining all kinds of horrible things that could've happened. Why haven't you at least returned my texts? So don't you just 'hey, girl' me…"

I turned to face her, giving her my most sincere smile. "Hope, I'm sorry. I've been a terrible friend and I admit that." I could see her start to argue, but then her nose wrinkled up as she glanced at the pan on the stove.

"What is that? It smells amazing."

"It's the topping for a cheesecake I'm making."

Her smile brightened, and she clapped her hands gleefully in front of her. "For me? Oh my, you know I love cheesecake. Is this your way of saying sorry? Because you didn't have to do that, but you know, I'm glad you did."

"Um…well…you know, to be honest?" I began, only to be cut off by the sudden ringing of my cell phone. A quick glance revealed a number I was familiar with. I held up a single finger to Hope, letting her know that I had to take this call as I scooped up the phone and walked into the living room.

"Hello, this is Allie," I said.

"Allie, it's Isla. Isla Garner."

"Hello Dr. Garner. How is she?" I asked, chewing on my lower lip just enough to hopefully keep my nerves out of my voice.

"Well, that's what I'm calling about. Just wanted you to know that she's recovering at a remarkable rate. She's just regained consciousness and has shifted back into her human form. She's in a lot of pain and I'm going to give her some meds, but if you wanted to speak with her I think now's a good time."

"Okay, no problem. I'll be there in five." I hung up and rushed into the kitchen. Thankfully, the timer for the cheesecake was just going off. I carefully removed it from the oven and placed it on the large center island to cool. Turning off the burner heating the reduction, I turned to face Hope. "I'm sorry, but right now is not a good time. I hate to do this but I really have to run... We'll finish this conversation as soon as I'm done with his errand. I promise."

I rushed toward the door, grabbing up my keys on the way.

"Oh no, hold up," said Hope, following closely behind me. "I came all the way over here to discuss things with you, and I'll be damned if I let you just run out halfway through."

I climbed into the driver seat of my car almost at the same time that Hope wedged herself into the passenger seat.

"Wherever you're going, I'm going too, because something tells me we have a lot of shit to talk about." She fastened her seatbelt and turned to face me, her features set in a way that let me know her actions were not up for discussion. "So. Where we going?"

I didn't have the time or the energy to argue with her. "Fine. We're heading to the vet."

Minutes later, we screeched to a halt in front of Dr. Garner's office. I had given Hope the thirty-second elevator pitch as to what had happened the night before.

"Girl, how you get messed up in stuff like this?" she had asked, just as we pulled up. "How do you go from serving coffee and doing some fake tarot readings for tourists, to hanging out with werewolves and... cat people, or whatever you called her."

"Panther. She's a Were-Panther. A Shifter, like Cody. And she was helping us train to catch a vampire." On that note, I parked and stepped out of the car. Hope exited slowly, never once taking her eyes off me as we entered the veterinarian's office.

I rushed into the lobby, nearly running into Esmay, who had been straightening the furniture in the reception area.

"Allie," she said coolly.

"Hi, Esmay. This is my friend Hope. Is Dr. Garner in the back?"

She nodded and motioned for us to go on through. I tried to smile at her as we walked past, but quickly cast my eyes aside as I got nothing in return.

"Your bill is seventeen hundred dollars," Esmay said to my back. "For the doctor's time and supplies from last night. I'll also be adding on all of the missed revenue from us having to stay closed to business today to take care of your friend."

Bitch. That was what I wanted to say as I paused, but then thought better of it. She was right. If it weren't for us, they would probably be seeing paying customers right about now. Rather than acknowledge any of that, I pushed open the door and walked into the surgical bay. The room was spotless and clean in that sterile way that only medical spaces could attain. The metal operating table that last night had been covered in Kendra's blood now sat empty.

"She's resting in one of the recovery rooms." I jumped at the sound of the voice, and turned to see Dr. Garner had entered the room with us. She nodded for us to join her, and she turned and walked farther down the hall.

I quickened my stride to keep up with the doctor. "Is she conscious? Is she going to be okay?" She turned to face me and seemed to be on the verge of saying something, but then pursed her lips together tightly as she glanced at Hope. "Dr. Garner, please, I need to know. This is my best friend, and I have hidden too much from her already. Everything needs to come out into the open."

She sighed and smiled stiffly at the two of us. "Isla. Please, call me Isla. Your friend is doing much better, considering the shape she was in and how much blood she lost. I have always heard that Shifters possess amazing recuperative abilities. But had I not seen this with my own eyes, I would never have believed it; she was literally on the brink of death. She's still weak and I recommend that she stay here for the rest of the day, but she can go home in the morning. I don't see any reason that she won't make a full recovery. However, keep your conversation as short as possible and try not to tax her."

She pushed open the door at the end of the hall and motioned for us to follow her. Before I could go through, Hope grabbed me by the elbow, spinning me around to face her.

"So are you saying vampires are real?" she whispered, her face a mask of confusion.

"What? Is that what you're focused on? We'll talk about that later..."

The space we entered was sparsely furnished. A single chair, a dressing table pressed to one wall, and the stretcher on which Kendra lay were the only items in the room. She had been dressed in a hospital gown, and a single thin sheet covered her to just above her breast. Her hair was disheveled and her Mediterranean-toned skin actually seemed pale—but that could've been the atrocious track lighting that shone down on her. When she opened her eyes, however, they were as bright and attentive as ever.

I stood next to the bed and reached a hand under the sheet to clasp hers. Her smile was weak, yet seemed genuine and warm. Granted, I had not known her for very long, but her honesty and openness had quickly endeared her to me. I could feel my eyes welling up, and I had to blink quickly to keep the tears at bay.

"Kendra. I am so sorry."

"Sorry?" she said, her voice harsh and strained. "What are you sorry for? You didn't shoot me."

But maybe if I hadn't been there, no one else would have shot you either.

Instead of saying those words, I gave her hand a small squeeze and forced a tight smile. "Kendra, do you remember what happened?"

She leaned back against the pillow and closed her eyes. "It all happened so fast. I remember smelling the fires while I was still in the woods with you and Cody. I shifted and sprinted to the encampment. All hell was breaking loose when I arrived, but I caught the scent of someone that definitely did not belong in the camp. Something about their smell made me so angry; it wasn't the actual scent itself but what it was mixed with. It smelled like…and I'm sorry I don't have any other way to put this…it smelled the way that old, decaying flesh tastes. It was something rotten and overlaid with black magic."

I gritted my teeth; what she was describing was a smell and a feeling I knew only too well. I nodded and urged her to continue.

"I looked around for the source of the stench and saw two men near the back of the encampment. They had a plastic gas container and were sprinkling a line of gasoline behind a row of tents. I think they intended to create some sort of break line behind everyone so that no one could escape the fire. Everything they were doing screamed 'evil', and every instinct I had told me to kill. I knew I shouldn't have, but I couldn't stop myself. I charged at the two men, giving myself over to all the rage I was feeling."

She turned her head to the side, swallowing hard. I remembered what the doctor had said and wondered if maybe we had talked enough, but before I could voice my concerns she turned her head to face us and continued.

"I've never felt anything like it. It was blind fury, and I could practically taste their blood on my fangs as I leapt at them. But they were ready for me. The one without the gas can spun around and threw some type of powder in my face. I remember feeling like I was suffocating, that no matter how hard I tried I couldn't get any oxygen into my lungs. And then, just like that, I shifted back into my human form."

Shock caused me to interrupt. "Wait, you mean they were able to make you Shift against your will?"

"Yes. Until that moment, I had thought that was something only magic can accomplish. But this didn't feel like magic. Whatever that powder was, it felt like it numbed my brain. Like it just flipped a switch inside me...but not in a mystical sense. I think this was science."

"What happened after that?" I asked.

"Being shoved back into my human form like that was a shock to my system. I felt weak and disoriented, and that was when the same man hit me very hard across the face. I went down, stunned, still unable to completely process what was happening. Then he kicked me, rolling me over onto my back. I could see both of them standing over me, looking down and smiling. I remember one of them saying something like, 'Okay, that works... Let's see if this one will as well.' I heard the cock of a gun, and could just make out the barrel of a pistol that was pointed at me. Before he pulled the trigger, his partner leaned down close and said, 'You are about to die, Kitty, but in case you don't: tell your friends that Mallis is coming, and he's bringing about the Leveling.' And that was it. There was a flash, a loud bang, and suddenly my stomach was on fire. That's all I remember before waking up here."

Dr. Garner entered the room with a small syringe that she hooked up to Kendra's IV bag. She pushed a clear fluid through the line and then made some adjustments to the monitoring equipment at her bedside.

"I'm just given her another bolus of antibiotics," she said. "Not that she needs it, but better to be safe than sorry with the type of wound that she had. Speaking of which..." She rolled Kendra's sheet down just enough to examine the bandage across her stomach. "No bleeding. That's good. Actually it's remarkable, but given everything I've seen from her in the last couple of hours, I'm not surprised."

"Dr. Garner... I mean Isla, do you have a sample of her blood from when she first came in?" I asked.

"Well, considering that she bled through just about every gauze we had, yeah, there's plenty of it around. Why?"

"Can you run some tests on her blood? She said that the man who shot her threw something in her face, and when she breathed it in it caused her to shift to her human form. I have no idea what you'd be looking for, but maybe there's something in her blood that can at least give us an idea of what she was exposed to."

"You think this was some kind of a dry run?" Kendra asked. "That whoever these men are, whoever they're working for, they're probing us for weaknesses?"

"Not just weaknesses, Kendra; I think they're looking for ways to kill Shifters. A chemical that makes them shift into human form combined with silver bullets? Someone knows what they're doing."

"It has to be this Mallis character," she added. "Whoever—or whatever—he is, he seems to be behind this."

"Agreed," I said. "Kendra, what they said about the Leveling, do you know what that is?"

"No idea. I've never heard that term before."

"I have." We all turned at the sound of the voice to face Esmay where she was standing, just inside the doorway. Her eyes were wide, and she was obviously shaken by what she had heard.

"Esmay, babe...what is it?" Isla said.

"The Leveling. It's a term used by the most ancient of vampires. It refers to one of their old myths about a spell that is capable of blotting out the sun."

Chapter Seven

The look on her face might have screamed surprise and anxiety, but her voice was strong and steady.

"Esmay," said Dr. Garner, "what are you talking about?"

"The Leveling," Esmay continued, "it's a bullshit myth. One that's nearly been lost to obscurity over time. It was something that the Elders told to the newborns to give them hope that one day they could be rulers of this world."

"Maybe we should continue this conversation outside," said Dr. Garner, glancing over her shoulder at Kendra.

"No way," said Kendra. "Whatever's going on here, I'm the one that was shot for it."

I glanced at Isla and shrugged. Kendra was right; these bastards had used her as target practice, and there was no way was I letting them get away with that. If what Esmay had to say could help me find them, then Kendra deserved to hear it as well.

"First of all," I said, "how do you know about any of this?"

She took a deep breath, cocking her head at Isla, who just shrugged and nodded. "You might say that supernatural things are in my blood; or rather, in my bloodline. This type of knowledge has been my family's business, going back seven generations."

As she was talking I sent out a tiny, tendril of magic to probe her. To my surprise, she turned to look at me.

"As you can see, Allie, I'm human." I withdrew the magic as my cheeks burned, and I refused to make eye contact with Isla. "Just because I have knowledge of something, it doesn't mean I'm one of them." Okay, that stung, and I tried not to show it. "I'm sorry. That was uncalled for. I just get very defensive when it comes to talking about my family."

"Go ahead, tell her," urged Isla.

"I was born into a long line of hunters," said Esmay.

"What did they hunt?" said Hope. I had all but forgotten she was even in the room. Her voice sounded small coming from the corner where she stood, arms folded across her body.

"Mostly goblins, trolls, dark elves, and other creatures that found their way into this realm from the Fae world; things that would feed upon human children for the most part. But occasionally, we would cross paths with Shifters and pixies as well." She glanced at Hope as if reading her mind. "Yes, they do exist. They're rare, but they are out there."

"Pixies?" asked Hope, arching her eyebrows.

"Yes. They are far nastier than you might think."

"But..." I could tell Hope had gotten a little overwhelmed by all of this. "But...they are so cute. I mean, Tinkerbell was a pixie, right?"

"Tinkerbell was a psychotic, homicidal bitch," replied

Esmay with no trace of irony in her voice. "Think about what kind of justice would be brought down on a human that did half the shit she did to Wendy."

"Do you kill Shifters?" said Kendra, a tightness working its way into her voice.

Esmay hesitated slightly, which told us all the answer. "I myself have not. But my family…yes, there have been times where Shifters have come across our paths and had to be put down. But trust me: there were reasons."

"You keep referring to your family. But what about you? What is your personal experience with all of this?" What I had wanted to ask her was what her experience with killing was.

"For the most part, my knowledge is only theoretical. I've been trained in combat with limited knowledge of certain types of Earth Magic and how they work. But my training was… interrupted… before I actually encountered any supernaturals one on one."

"Then what? We're just supposed to take you at your word about all of this?" I wasn't sorry I said it. I needed to know everything that Esmay knew.

"Back home, my parents had one of, if not the, largest private libraries dedicated to supernatural lore in the United States. I would spend hours there, reading everything I could get my hands on."

I couldn't fault her for that. I was doing the same back at my aunts' house. "Where's home?"

"Seattle. It's a hotbed of supernatural activity, much like Trinity Falls. Mount Rainier is an aging portal through which a lot of creatures from the dark realm find their way."

"That's how we met," said Isla. "I was doing a residency in Seattle at a clinic there, and Esmay brought in a stray kitten she found for a wellness visit. As cliché as it may sound, it really was love at first sight."

"And is that why you broke training with your family?" I asked. "I mean, you talk about them in the past tense, and you said your training was interrupted. Was Isla the interruption? Did your family not approve?"

"What? No, it was nothing like that," said Esmay. "My family loved Isla. Granted, they didn't like me getting involved with anyone at the time, regardless of their gender, because my training came first. But no, I left Seattle because..." She choked up, swallowing hard. Isla placed a reassuring hand on her lover's shoulder, giving her a quick squeeze. "I left because my brother and father were killed in an attack. They were taking out a nest of Shifters that had been snatching up children from one of the campsites near Rainier, and were taken by surprise by a particularly nasty clan of Bear-Shifters. They weren't prepared for what came at them...and died before they could call for help. That only left myself and my mother to carry on the family legacy of hunting. I told my mother that while I loved the education, discovering everything there was to know about magic and the supernatural, I was not a hunter at heart. After losing my father and brother, she was in no mood to argue with me. Instead, she sold the house and all of our belongings, gave me the money to start my own life, and sent me away."

I swallowed a hard lump in my throat before I dared to try speaking. "What happened to her?" It might not have been the most sensitive question I could have asked, but I had to know.

Esmay sighed, and I could see her eyes welling with long-held-back tears. "I have no idea. The last time I saw her, she took a crossbow and an Elvin knife, and headed for the hiking trails at the back of our old house that led to the deep woods outside of Seattle. I think she was going after the Shifters that killed our family. She wouldn't let me go with her, and the last thing I remember was her giving me a kiss goodbye...and then everything went dark. I woke up at Isla's house."

"She drugged you," said Isla. I could sense fresh anger in her voice, though she struggled valiantly to hold it at bay. "There was a knock at my door, and when I opened it you were collapsed on the porch. I took you inside and kept watch over you until you regained consciousness a few hours later. We went back to where you had last seen your mother, but she was nowhere to be found. A few days later, we left the States for Italy to start a new life somewhere far from Seattle and all the bad memories we left behind. When I heard about my aunt dying in a fire, we decided it was time to return to America and carve out a life for us here."

I felt a deep burn at the mention of her aunt. I knew that I'd have to tell Isla what really happened that night at some point, but this was definitely not the right time or place.

"I am so very sorry for your loss, Esmay. Truly." It was all I could manage to force out at the moment.

"Thank you," she answered. "That means a lot. But back to the questions at hand. While I have never known anyone to face an actual vampire, I am certain that they do exist. My family was certain of it as well. There was a lot of lore out there about them, including tomes dating back centuries, dedicated to tracking them throughout the ages. One of those tomes was the Necris Apolla. It detailed many of the dogma and rituals by which they were rumored to live. One of those beliefs was that there was a way for them to ascend to near godhood, allowing them to walk unfettered, with nothing to limit them or hold them back."

"Godhood?" said Hope. "What do you mean?"

"Vampires are the most ancient of supernaturals. They are also among the most powerful. Their creation is shrouded in mystery and lore, beyond the knowledge of even generations of hunters. While the legends of their powers seem to change depending on the source, there is one aspect that always remains the same: their vulnerability to sunlight."

"So then it stands to reason that if there was a way to remove that single vulnerability..." began Kendra.

"But is that their only vulnerability?" I asked. "There has to be more than one way to kill them."

"There has been talk handed down from other hunting clans. Beheading and then burning the head, sunlight, and extreme heat seem to be the consistent stories from what I've heard."

"What about crosses and wooden stakes to the heart?" asked Hope.

"Crosses are meant to bring peace of mind to the person about to be killed by one, I believe," replied Esmay. "And as for stakes to the heart? Good luck if you get close enough to one to try it—and in all honesty, I don't think anything driven through their heart is going to do much more than piss them off. Their hearts don't beat, they're dead organs, so I'm not sure what piercing them is supposed to do."

"What about their powers?" I asked.

Esmay nodded. She appeared happy to answer questions she might be a little more familiar with. "Very fast, incredibly strong, and they have the ability to regenerate damaged tissue almost instantaneously. Enhanced senses, especially that of smell, and they can manipulate their skeletal structure to a certain degree."

"Skeletal structure?" I asked.

"Yeah, they can elongate their arms to give themselves greater reach, twist their spines in obscene positions if needed, and project their nails to act as weapons. And, of course, there are the fangs. Incredibly sharp, retractable, and unbreakable from what I've heard and read. From all accounts those are their known powers. As for the rumored abilities possessed by some…hunters have reported that they can turn into smoke or mist as needed, that if you lock eyes with one they can command your will, they can turn into bats or wolves, and that in those forms they can control other bats and wolves. Flight has been reported, as well as the ability to walk through solid walls. How much of that is true, I have no way of knowing. But one thing is certain: the older the vampire, the more powerful they are. And your friend Mallis is one of the oldest on record."

"What about magic?" said Hope. "I mean, if they aren't especially vulnerable to physical harm, what about the stuff that Allie can do?"

"Well, I'm not exactly familiar with what she can do," replied Esmay, "but I do remember reading accounts where vampires were defeated by witches, and that they consider witches to be their only real threats. But again, those were spotty references and there were no details provided."

"If that is the case, then why is he going out of his way to collect witches?" I replied. "I mean, wouldn't he just kill us? From what we learned at the encampment, he is tracking us down for some other reason."

"To power the Leveling most likely," said Kendra, as she attempted to sit up in bed. "Something of that nature would take a ton of magic, right? Mallis has the Warlock to help him cast the spell, but from what I've heard, male Warlocks can't actually generate the magic themselves..."

"Of course," I murmured half to myself and half to the room. "If he really thinks there is a way to blot out the sun, then he's going to need a very powerful spell to do it, and for that he's going to need a very powerful witch to drain."

"Or witches," said Esmay.

"What?"

"Witches. Plural. He can find one powerful one, but that won't be easy. Instead, he can siphon off the power from a lot of lesser witches and use that."

"There haven't been covens of witches in Trinity Cove in decades," I said.

"No, but they are moving back to the area. Like the Shifters, they are drawn here," said Kendra. "I can feel their magic flowing...and if I can feel it, chances are good that the Warlock can as well. But I guess it's still a moot point. Feeling it is one thing; actually locating them is another. It's not like the Warlock has a map of where they all hang out."

Oh shit. Fuck me sideways.

"Allie?" Isla said, approaching me. "Are you okay? All the color just drained from your face."

I felt my legs go numb and I barely made it to the chair in the corner of the room before dropping down. "I'm such an idiot! I think I may have just created the map they needed."

Chapter Eight

"You did what?" said Hope.

"I thought I was helping. When they told us in the encampment that the Order was trying to round up witches, all I could think was that I had to find them first." It had seemed like the right thing to do at the time, but in hindsight, what I really thought was, How could I have been so stupid?

Oh no. Cody. I may have just put the man that I love in mortal danger. "Come on, Hope, we need to go!"

I promised Kendra that I would be back to check on her, but for now she was probably safest staying where she was. Plus, no matter how quickly she was healing, she was still injured. Dr. Garner agreed that it was best for her to remain at the clinic until tomorrow. I thanked Dr. Garner as we rushed out before turning to Esmay.

"Esmay, can I ask a favor of you?" I said.

She turned her head partially to the side, squinting at me. "Depends. What is it?"

"You still have access to the records kept by your family?"

"Everything is back home outside of Seattle. Like I said, my mother sold everything. However, I did box up a lot the books in the old library and put them in storage. I still have friends there; I can ask someone to ship me a couple of books overnight that might be of some help."

"That would be amazing. I just need anything more you can dig up—especially regarding Mallis—and any information on how the leveling might work."

I turned to leave the office, but she stopped me by grabbing my arm, forcing me to face her again.

"Hey, what about your tab? If we're keeping her here another night you'll really owe us."

"Esmay, please," began Dr. Garner.

I held up my hand to cut her off. "No, she's right. I do owe you. Um, but for right now will a cheesecake do? I meant to bring it over as a thank-you anyway."

"Hold up," said Hope, standing just outside the doorway. "You mean that cake wasn't for me?"

I just rolled my eyes and tossed the keys her way as we headed for the car.

"You drive. I've got to try and get ahold of Cody."

Hope climbed behind the wheel and started the engine as I fastened my seatbelt. "We going back to your house?"

"No," I answered. "Head for Cody's. I'm going to try him on his cell phone. He lives off of Plaza Avenue near Center City."

I had the phone to my ear even as we were pulling away from the veterinary clinic. There was no answer, and his phone rang and rang before a monotonous voice informed me that I had reached his number, followed by Cody stating his name and urging me to leave a message.

"Cody, it's Allie. I need you to call me as soon as you get this. I think I've really fucked up."

I could sense Hope stealing glances at me, but I couldn't bring myself to meet her eyes. Instead, I stabbed at the screen on my phone, sending Cody the same message via text.

"Allie, I'm sure he's fine. I mean, he's a deputy and he's a werewolf. I'm sure he can handle himself."

I hoped so. I didn't want to think about the potential danger I had possibly put him in. I sighed deeply, pinching the bridge of my nose in a vain attempt to ward off an impending headache. "Of course he can take care of himself—under normal circumstances. But you haven't seen what the Order can do." I stopped short of mentioning our encounter with the She-Wolf, shuddering at the thought of Cody coming up against her by himself.

"I'm sorry, Allie. But this is all some weird shit that you've gotten yourself tangled up in. I just don't want to see anything happen to you. I don't pretend to understand what you're going through, and I don't want you to feel like you have to explain it all. Just know that you're my friend and I got your back. Well, unless there are vampires involved, 'cause I ain't trying to get down with that."

I couldn't help but laugh. She had done the impossible and taken my mind off Cody. I started to reply with something witty when my phone buzzed once in my hand. Text message. I read it and breathed a sigh of relief.

"What is it?"

"It's from Cody. He's fine, just stuck in a meeting at the precinct. Can't talk right now." I quickly pounded out a message telling him not to go back to his place, but to bring the map back to my house as soon as he could, and that I would explain once he was there. "No need to keep going to his place. I've asked him to meet me at home. Turn around; let's head back."

Hope almost seemed relieved as she signaled and turned into a bank parking lot to swing back around.

"Hope, is it just me, or do you not like Cody?"

I could see her white-knuckling the steering wheel as she eased us back into traffic. "Honestly, I don't know him. At least not the way a person should know her best friend's new beau. I can't make a decision based on 'oh great, your boyfriend didn't maul you tonight'. Granted, it's not fair for you to ask me something like that when one of the few times I've been around him he turned into a giant dog and tore my house up."

"Wolf. He turned into a wolf, and he saved us both at your house." I sunk back into the seat, feeling a little sullen. "Okay, and maybe he broke a few things…but on the bright side, we didn't die."

For some reason, that set us both into a laughing fit. It felt good, and I had to remind myself that it was okay to take a moment and give in to the feeling of happiness, despite all the horror that had happened in the last few days.

"I will say," said Hope, "that he is fine to look at—when he is upright on two legs…" This threw me into another bout of laughter, and I rolled down my window to get some fresh air on my face. "But Allie, in all honesty, there is something I need to know."

I braced myself and turned my head toward my best friend. "Anything."

"Are you really going to give the cheesecake to that vet and her uppity girlfriend? 'Cause you know how I feel about some cake."

I couldn't contain my smile as we bantered back and forth on the way home.

We pulled into the driveway at my aunts' house, and I reached out slightly with my mind to touch the wards that danced all around our home. Everything was as it should be; the only disturbance in them was a familiar one. Gar was home, and I could tell that he was alone.

As soon as we entered the door, I tossed my keys aside and bolted the door behind Hope. As soon as it was secured, I set the alarm and whispered the wards back into place. We had already decided that the cheesecake wasn't going to make it back to the vet's office, so it was fair game for Hope. Tomorrow was another day and I could bake a second cake at that point; I figured this would be a great gesture toward letting Hope know that she was still my Number One Bitch.

"Gar," I called out, unsure exactly where he was. "Come have some cheesecake with me and Hope!"

I cocked my head, listening for an answer that didn't come. The stairwell was dark leading downstairs as Hope set out some dessert plates and glasses. The large basement was quiet. The usual greeting of rumbling tanks and machine gun fire from my brother's PlayStation didn't greet me as I expected.

"Gar?" I called again, looking around the space. The bathroom door was slightly ajar and I could see he wasn't in there, and the second, smaller kitchen did not look disturbed. On a whim, I stepped out onto the lower level deck to check for him.

There was a large L-shaped teak sofa and chair set at

one end of the deck, but the other side had a hanging cocoon style chair suspended by a metal chain, floating about three feet above the deck. That was where I found him, sitting cross-legged in the chair and gazing out over the plunging backyard that led to the edge of the woods.

"Gar? I was calling you. Didn't you hear me?"

He remained quiet, his gaze locked on something in the distance. The slight breeze in the air was barely enough to cause a whispering of the chimes suspended on one of our neighbors' decks. I bit my lip, worried that maybe something was wrong with him, and I debated brushing him with magic to probe for any signs of sickness. Before I could decide, he looked over at me, his eyes puffy and red. Was he…crying?

"Gar? Hey, what is it? Are you okay?" I pulled one of the smaller chairs from a bar table at the back of the deck, and bought it over so I could sit facing my brother.

"I heard you calling. I just wanted to be alone for a bit."

I hesitated, taking in what he said and the tone in his voice. "Do you want to talk about it?"

He sighed, turning away to again gaze at something I couldn't see. "If I ask you something, will you tell me the truth?"

"Of course I will, Gar. We've gotten past all that, remember? What is it?"

He swallowed hard and turned to look at me again. "Did you see Mom?"

The little voice was screaming in the back of my mind: Lie! Lie! I swallowed hard and kindly told it to shut the fuck up, then nodded.

"I did. But it wasn't the mom that we remember, Gar."

"That's easy for you to say, Allie, because you remember her. I don't!" The tears were rolling again as he reached one hand up to smear them away, never once taking his eyes off the tree line at the edge of our property. "What was she like?"

"Her voice was the same as ever...and I could make out her—"

"No," Gar interrupted, "I mean what did she look like? Was she a ghost?"

I hesitated, not sure how much to actually say. "Gar, if you're asking...Mom died. I'm not sure when, but what I met was her shade, her spirit. That was all that was left of her. She was guarding the forbidding that she created to keep a very nasty Warlock locked away. It wasn't like she could have returned to us."

He contemplated my words, tears still flowing down his cheeks. "But you got to see her; to feel her, Allie. I wish I could have been there."

"No, you don't. Trust me, it wasn't what you might be imagining. It was terrible and cold...and I think she was so ready to go. She seemed...tired."

"Did she say anything? Did she ask about me or say why she left us?"

This time I didn't hesitate. "She said that she misses and loves you very much. That leaving us was her greatest regret but that she did what she had to do in order to protect us." I almost felt guilty until he looked at me, relief washed across his soft features.

"Really?" He couldn't hide the fact that he wanted my words to be the truth, and it nearly brought me to tears.

"Really," I said, reaching up to rub the side of his face and then ruffle his hair. It brought a smile to his face, which in turn lightened mine. "One thing, Gar. Where did you hear about this?"

"Jhamal. He works part-time for his aunt at the veterinary clinic, helping to clean the rooms and cages. He overheard his aunt and her girlfriend talking with someone last night. Someone, he said, that you brought into the clinic for help. Why would you bring a human to a pet doctor?"

"That's a long story, and one we can get into another time. Right now...are you sure I can't interest you in some of that cake before Hope finishes it off?"

He grinned and nodded. "Oh! And can you believe that Doctor Garner is gay! And her girlfriend is so hot! I guess we really are everywhere!"

I laughed as he rushed into the house. Something he just said stuck in the back of my mind for some reason. We really are everywhere.

Before I could decode what it meant, my phone buzzed. It was Cody.

"Allie! I think you need to get over to my place now!"

Chapter Nine

I tried not to wreck my car or get a ticket as I sped across town to Cody's small two-bedroom house. It had taken everything I had to downplay why I was leaving to Hope and Gar. If they thought I was half as panicked as I felt, they would have insisted on coming with me, and that was something I didn't want to deal with. I was worried enough about Cody. His tone was strained, but didn't sound like he was in any type of danger—just a little stressed, which was unusual for him.

I wasn't sure what I might be walking into, and the fear of the unknown caused my stomach to twist into knots. I willed my body to calm down, and tried focusing on my magic while I drove. It was there, coiled like a serpent ready to strike at my command. But I was getting worn out from constantly having to tap into my magic like this. Maybe it was my concern for Cody that was the tipping point. I suddenly realized the strain I was putting on myself. I was tired in my bones. I was tired of causing pain and grief for the ones I loved. I was tired of always worrying when the next mystical shoe was going to drop. I was tired of worrying if the decision I had just made was the wrong one or the right one. Mostly, I was just tired of feeling like my life had spiraled out of control over the last few months; like someone else was driving my bus, and I was just a passenger pulling at a "stop here" cord that wasn't working.

None of this was anything I had asked for. Yeah, magic had seemed like a fun idea back when it didn't carry any weight. But now, it was like a boulder tied to my waist as I waded into the ocean.

Cody lived just south of Trinity Cove in a funky little Art Deco area called The Centrals. It was an enclave comprised of eclectic industrial lofts and small single-family mid-century houses. For years, the area had been crawling with drug addicts, thieves, and vagrants. Even though it had long since undergone gentrification, the stigma about the area, and its proximity to the train tracks and highways, kept rental prices down. Roughly a decade ago, artists and musicians discovered the area and fell in love with the buildings. Low rent meant that they could focus on their art without the worry of the eviction, and they were now the main inhabitants.

Cody was the first—and to my knowledge, the only—police officer to live in The Centrals. It had taken a couple years for his neighbors to trust him, but after a while they grew to accept him in their midst. Plus, they realized that having a cop living next door was a good deterrent for some of the crimes of opportunity by which they were occasionally plagued.

I pulled into the gravel driveway of the ranch-style home he had purchased after graduating from the police academy. It was an unassuming red brick house with a concrete sidewalk that led to a tiny front stoop. The canary yellow door complemented the brightly colored flower pots arranged on either side of it, overflowing with a variety of greenery. I reached for the buzzer but stopped short as I realized the door had been forced; the jamb was splintered in places where it had been rent open by brute strength.

I pulled up my magic and sent it swirling around my hand, ready to blast anyone that popped up in my way. Rather than announce myself, I pushed open the door and tried to enter the house as quietly as possible.

I sent a wave of magic ahead of me to probe for anyone that might be lurking deeper in the dwelling. It was a small house comprised of a combination sitting and living room, with a kitchen leading to a sunporch behind that. Off to one side was a narrow corridor that led to the two bedrooms, with a hall bathroom between them. It might not have been the largest, but it was still plenty big enough to hide a nasty surprise or two.

My magical probe hummed at me just as I was about to pass by the hallway leading to the kitchen. I spun to face the corridor, and raised my fist to send a blistering wave of magic at whatever was standing there.

"Whoa, whoa, it's me!" said Cody, raising one arm to shield his face.

I stopped the blast before I could release it and pulled the magic back into me. My head buzzed at the effort of recalling the attack, but it was nothing compared to what Cody would have felt had I unleashed a full blast of hellish magical fury at him.

I threw my body against his and wrapped my arms around him. "Cody, I told you to come to my house right away! What happened?"

He chuckled softly and hugged me back. "Hey, what's happening here? I can feel your heart trip-hammering!"

"I thought you were dead."

He pushed me back, holding me nearly at arm's length as he looked me in the eyes. "Dead? What would've made you think that? I had to come back here because I needed to water my orchids. Then I was going to grab a few things and head over. When I got here, I found my door kicked in and I caught a whiff of…the same dark magic I could smell at the Shifter camp. But only a hint of it." He took me by the hand and led me down the narrow corridor to the very back bedroom that he used as a home office. "Everything in the house was okay except for this…" He pushed open the office door so that I could peek inside.

The room looked like it had been hit by a tornado. Papers were strewn everywhere, books were tossed off their shelves, and his desk drawers had been pulled out completely, their contents thrown all over the small room.

"What…what happened here?" was all I could manage.

"This is the only room they hit. Whatever they wanted, they thought it would be in here. It makes no sense. My cash, watch, and two guns are still in my bedroom—it doesn't look like they even went in there. Why would someone who smells of dark magic trash my office?"

The light in the back of my mind went off and then started flashing in an angry red warning pattern. "The map, Cody! Where is it?"

"It's locked in the glove compartment of my car. Do you think that's what they were after?"

I told him what I had inadvertently done by creating that map, and could see the light of realization firing in his eyes as I spoke.

"But," he said, when I had finished, "the map is still only a generalization. It doesn't give them the specific addresses of any supernaturals. However, I think I may have solved that."

Together, we walked out to the sunporch and into the carport that shaded his car. He unlocked the passenger side and opened the glove box. Inside was indeed the map I had created, but paper-clipped behind it were another couple of pages I didn't recognize.

"You hit on something when you asked about tracking down anyone new in these areas that might stand out. I searched the county records division, property liens, and municipals records until I found a pattern that repeated in each of these areas you marked."

"What was the pattern?" I asked.

"No digital trail. Everything at each of the addresses I printed out is paid only in cash. No mortgage or automatic debits for rent. All utilities are paid in cash each month. There are no cable, internet or streaming services listed for these addresses either. If they have mobile phones, I'm betting they are all Go-Phones on a cash-pay plan. Basically, whoever lives at these residences are…ghosts, for all intents and purposes."

I nodded. What he was saying made sense. "Perfect for someone that may need to disappear at a moment's notice and leave no trace."

"Exactly. It's pretty much the same M.O. as the members of the Shifter encampment. No ties to a community."

"That could be good and bad for them," I said. "With no records of who they really are, if they were to disappear…"

"Or be recruited away…" added Cody.

"There would be no one to report them missing, and no way for the police to track them down."

"Exactly. And I'm betting the few names that were tied to the records are fictitious. They all moved into the area within the last few months."

"Bingo," I said. "We still have no idea if these are Shifters, witches or what. But since we know the Order is looking for witches, but also trying to recruit more Shifters, it stands to reason that they don't care who they get…either way, it's a win."

"So that explains what they wanted inside my house. They didn't get the map, and wouldn't be able to make the connections I made, so we are still a couple of steps ahead of them. What is our next move?"

I tried to ignore the hitch I felt in my chest at those words. I had known they were coming, and if I was being honest with myself, I had dreaded hearing them. Truth be told, I did have an idea, but doubt nagged at me, threatening to drag me down like that damn boulder tied to my waist.

"Let's head back in and grab whatever you need before we head back to my place for supplies."

"Supplies? Do you have a plan?"

"I have the beginnings of a plan. But before we can do anything, I need to make sure that everyone on that list is safe." I nodded at the sheets of paper Cody was folding and stuffing into his pockets.

He frowned, not loving what I had just said. "How are you going to do that, Allie?"

I took a deep breath and gave him the most confident look I could muster. "I'm going to cast protective wards around their homes. Like the ones at my aunts' house and the one I placed around Hope's. Only stronger. I'm going to cast a ward that will repel any supernatural being that gives off even a hint of that black magic the Order and its army are emitting."

"Can you do that?"

I maintained my same confidence and nodded. "I can now. I'm a hell of a lot stronger than I used to be." I turned to head back into Cody's house, and my smile fell away as soon as he could no longer see my face. Yes, I was stronger, but I had no idea if I was strong enough to pull this off. The fact was, this wasn't really what I had planned, but in order to pull off part two, I had to make sure that any witches or Shifters that were living in town were safe. That was why they had flocked to Trinity: to find refuge and to be with their own kind again. Now, I had to make sure things stayed that way for them. Only then would I tell Cody what I had in mind.

Hopefully, it wouldn't get us both killed.

Chapter Ten

"But I don't get it. Why, Allie?"

I didn't have the time or the energy to argue with Gar. Things were about to get messy and complicated, and I didn't need to worry about protecting him.

"Because I'm asking you to, Gar, that's why. Look, it's only for tonight, and maybe tomorrow. I need you to go and stay at Hope's house, okay?"

"Right. Because I'm useless to you."

"What? No, that's not true. I can't focus on taking out a Warlock and a vampire and worry about you too. It's as simple as that."

"You know, it's not my fault I was born normal!" I could see his eyes beginning to well up, and he had to ball his hands into fists to keep them from trembling.

"Gar...is that what you think? Do you think I see you as someone less than me? Less than Cody?" My voice wavered now, and it was my turn to try to hold back tears. "You are my brother and I love you. I would do anything to protect you…no matter if you were born the most powerful witch in existence, or born just Gar. Because in the end, that's what you are to me; my Gar. And I will never let anything hurt you." I grabbed him and hugged him and we both succumbed to our tears.

"I just think that maybe if I had been born special like you, I could have seen Mom one last time as well. Maybe I could have helped you…maybe together we would have been able to save her." His voice sounded weak and ragged as he sobbed into my shoulder.

And there it was. Despite all the horrors I had been through in the last few days, nothing held a candle to those that were bred in the dark corners of a young boy's mind—a young boy who missed his mother and felt guilty that he couldn't save her. The fact that he never really knew her didn't matter. In his mind, he had created a fantasy world where we were still one big happy family—or, more likely, where she would come waltzing back through the door one day, and we would pick up where we left off.

What I had provided was proof that that was never going to happen.

"Gar. I am so sorry you are going through this. But I promise you, being in that cave…seeing what I saw…it's the last thing our mother would have wanted. You have to believe me on that one." I broke our embrace just enough to take his face in both hands and look him in the eyes. "Our mother loved us. Both of us. She did what she had to in order to make sure that we could live as long and as full lives as possible. If she could see the young man you have become, she would be overcome with pride. I know that because that's how I feel every time I see you. She would want the same thing for you that I do: for you to live. And while you might not like the things I tell you, I swear it's because I have nothing but your best interests in mind. Do you believe that?"

He nodded, reaching to embrace me once again.

"I just..." he started, clearing his voice, "I just don't want you to end up like Mom. You're all I have, and I can't stand the thought that you might just disappear one day as well."

Not going to lie. That one nearly broke me. I cried hard with my little brother before I found the strength to look him in the eyes again. "Not gonna happen. I promise you. I'm never going to leave you."

I threw an arm around his shoulder before punching at him playfully. I offered up a silent prayer to whatever gods might be listening to make that last lie a truth.

In the end, I agreed that it was okay for Gar to stay with Jhamal for the evening. I made a mental note to check in with Jhamal's parents in the very near future—assuming I was still alive, that is—to get to know them and find out just what they knew about their son's "friendship" with my brother. Gar had always been evasive on the subject whenever I had suggested that we get together with Gar's family and make an evening of it. Oh well. I would cross that bridge when we came to it. I was just happy that he had agreed to stay somewhere out of the way until Cody and I had completed Phases One and Two of my plan.

When it came to reassuring her that I would make it through, Hope was nearly as difficult as Gar. I told her that I would call her as soon as it was safe. To thank her for taking Gar to his boyfriend's house, I gave her the rest of the cheesecake. I knew she really wanted it anyway, and to be honest, her friendship was infinitely more important to me than was making peace with Esmay. Besides, I loved baking; it relaxed me. I could always whip up another one if I survived the night.

"Okay, that was rough," said Cody, coming up behind me as I stood at the door, watching Hope drive away with my brother. "Are you okay?"

"I have to be," I said, steeling my voice. Cody's wince almost made me regret my reply. I turned to face him, placing one hand on his chest before stretching up to give him a kiss. "I'm sorry. I'm just a little stressed. I feel like I'm constantly behind the eight ball here, and every decision I make is…questionable, to say the least."

"But you're not giving up. We're not giving up. You're not alone in this. Not to toot my own horn, but my shoulders are pretty broad. I can handle some of that weight."

I felt myself blushing as we walked back through the house. This was scaring me too. On top of everything else, I had started to develop some very deep feelings for this man. Here I was, floundering my way through all kinds of unfamiliar territory in my life. And in some ways, I was less afraid of Mallis than I was of facing whatever was happening with Cody.

The thought of Mallis snapped me back to reality.

Cody must have read my mind. "Do we have everything you need?"

"Yep. You go downstairs and double check that the doors are all locked, and I'll grab one last thing from my room."

I stepped into my bedroom, and went to the top shelf in the very back of my walk-in closet. There was an old cigar box there, and inside were mementos I had collected as a child. Inside were a few odd feathers, and a couple of sea shells that I remember picking up on our summer trips to the beach. For the most part, however, the box was filled with an assortment of rocks and crystals that I had found over years of traipsing through the woods and hiking trails surrounding Trinity Cove. Sea glass, obsidian, clear crystal, grey river rock, and all types of different stones decorated the inside of the box.

I took a scarf that was hanging from one of the belt hooks on the wall, and folded it around all the tiny stones, creating a tiny pouch just for them. I hastily emptied a messenger bag that I had not used since my first attempt at going to college and placed the parcel inside. Slinging it obliquely across my shoulder, I headed out to meet Cody in the living room.

"Nice look," he said, eyeing the bag. "Very Lara Croft."

I smirked in response. "Har har. Move your ass before I decide to leave you here."

He laughed without realizing that I was only half joking.

Cody drove, and I focused on what needed to be done. I had researched everything I could find in my aunts' study about erecting wards and barriers. A ward is put in place as an early warning system. It lets the caster know that someone—or something—has stepped through them. A barrier, on the other hand, is completely different. It is designed to repel whatever the caster has deemed non-passable. I wanted to create a sort of hybrid of these two conjurings. I wanted to know when something passed through, but I also had to build a very specific type of shield: one that would allow the undisturbed passage of the owners, those to whom they give permission, and normal humans to come and go, but would act as a forcefield for anything supernatural that wasn't related to the family inside.

That would include She-Wolves and vampires, I hoped.

Casting a ward is pretty standard stuff. I had done it plenty of times lately. But casting a barrier requires a use of magic that was new to me. There are four different types of barriers, each corresponding to the four elements. They are driven by the caster's will, and their extent of power depends on how well the caster has bonded with the element from which the barrier came.

From what I had read, the Fire barrier was the most powerful, but also the most dangerous to create. It could flare out of control and do serious damage to the family inside if I wasn't careful. That, and the fact that my only experiences with fire—I could still feel it searing my lungs—didn't leave me feeling the most confident about it, so I nixed that option.

Air was too ephemeral for me. It was effective in keeping out spirits and ghostly manifestations, but it wasn't particularly effective against brute force.

That left Water and Earth. Water would have worked well, but I needed to tie the barrier to its element in the world…and a source of flowing water was too far away to be practical.

So, by process of elimination, I chose Earth. This was fine by me; it was the element with which I was most familiar, and the one I felt the most comfortable trying to manipulate. To create an Earth barrier, I needed crystals or rocks that were native to the region in which I was going to cast, and they had to be clean. "Clean" meant they could not have been clouded by another's aura or magic. The stones I had in my closet had been there undisturbed for years. They were as clean as any I could find. All my life I had loved hiking the falls, visiting beaches and remote mountain lakes with my aunts and Gar while building my little collection of crystals and rocks. Maybe it was a subconscious effort of preparing for this moment—who knows? All I knew was that I had enough to act as anchors for the spell I was about to create.

We approached the first house, located in an area north of Trinity Cove. It was a brick and vinyl split level set back from the road, with a considerable amount of land between it and the closest neighbor. This was a common thing, I realized as the day wore on. Apparently, supernaturals liked their privacy.

Cody eased the car to a stop and pointed at the small brick house before us. "That's it. Do I need to go all the way up to the house?"

"No. The less attention we attract, the better." I reached into my bag and took out the first stone I grabbed. It was one of the smooth, gray, river rocks. I held it in my hand and closed my eyes, centered my breathing, and grounded myself. I willed all my anxiety and nervous energy away, and instead reached into the stone and searched for the power that was innately connected to Mother Earth.

I felt it there, thrumming steadily in a way that reassured me, making me warm all over. All rocks that were not clouded by human energy were connected to the earth, and in this case, the ley lines that fed the bedrock of Trinity Cove. Once I found the magic within the stone, it was just a matter of calling it forth and shaping it to my will. I whispered age-old incantations into the stone, willing the power of the ley lines into action.

In my mind's eye, I could see the power flare to life. I reached out and grabbed it, commanding the mystical energy to do my bidding. I focused on the name of the owner of the establishment, just like the manuals had instructed, and raised the magical barrier. I commanded it to repel any supernatural beings who meant harm to the one true owner of the property.

When I was satisfied that the barrier was ready, I casually walked along the road until I was close enough to the house to toss the stone inside the property line. It landed harmlessly among the rock bedding of the small flower garden that lined the sidewalk leading to the home's front door. No one else would have noticed it, but to me, the barrier that sprang up and enveloped the house was like a shimmering blue dome: tall and strong and, hopefully, impregnable.

I climbed back into the car.

"All set?" Cody asked. "You look a little...exerted."

"What?" I flipped down the passenger's side visor to look in the mirror. I didn't realize that I had broken a sweat working up that spell. My skin looked a little clammy and my eyes were slightly puffy. "Yeah. I guess that took a little more out of me than I was expecting. But I feel fine."

Honestly, I felt better than fine. Magic was flowing through me, whispering and calling for me to use it again and again. Good thing I wasn't wiped, because I had to do this about a dozen more times today.

"So," said Cody as he eased the car back onto the road, heading to our next destination, "what do we do after you've set all these wards?"

"Simple," I replied, not daring to look at him. "We go

find these bastards and ask for a sit-down with them. Once I know the witches and Shifters in the community are safe, I want to broker a deal with the Warlock and Mallis. We are going to break bread, not heads."

Cody nearly ran off the side of the road as he whipped his head around to face me.

Chapter Eleven

"Look, it's not a big deal," I said. "For centuries, groups of people with different viewpoints have sat down together and come to an understanding. It's how civilization was born. Treaties are the backbone of...well, everything."

We were sitting at my coffee shop in town; I had needed to check on the employees and make sure everything was still in one piece. Cody and I decided to have some espresso and split one of my giant apple-and-cinnamon muffins.

There was a definite change in the clientele at the shop. Sure, the usual regulars were still there, but there was an unmistakable vibe of magic in the air; some of my new customers were not human. But everyone was having a good time, keeping to themselves or their small band of friends. The shop felt homey, and I liked that.

"Allie, I appreciate what you're saying. I really do, but this is a little different from The Treaty of Versailles," replied Cody.

"Is it? I mean, that was about bringing together various

nations and finding a resolution they could all be happy with and benefit from."

"Except that I don't think the Canadians had to worry that the Americans were going to turn into bloodthirsty wolves and vamps and kill them, or that their ultimate goal was to blot out the sun. That's a little different."

"First of all, a treaty is all about recognizing one another's differences and strengths so that they can find common ground. Who's to say there isn't common ground here? And also, I still think that whole Leveling thing is a myth; it's just a supernatural version of an urban legend."

"True. About the Leveling thing. But that makes me think, too. All legends are rooted in some form of truth. It may be exaggerated to a degree, but it has to have some kind of basis in fact. Who knows what it could really mean? Plus, you have seen the level of fanaticism the Order has to this Warlock; who knows to what level they worship Mallis? They probably have no interest in talking."

I sat back in my leather club chair and sipped my now lukewarm espresso. Cody could be right about everything he said, but I had to believe that talking it out was at least worth a try. I was tired of fighting, tired of being outsmarted, and tired of feeling afraid. I wanted to meet the monster hiding under my bed and ask it just what the fuck it was doing in my room.

"It's a gamble, Cody, but the worst that could happen is they laugh at us and say 'no deal.'"

"Uh, no. That's not the worst that could happen, and you know it. They could kill us. Or eat us alive. Or torture us for days on end. Or…"

"Okay, I get it. We could die. But what is the alternative? We stay the course? Keep reacting whenever they prod us? For years, Shifters and humans have lived side by side in peace. We need to find out what Mallis really wants, and maybe find a way to give him something that keeps him happy and everyone else safe. No one wants more bloodshed."

I hoped I was right, but part of me was afraid that was exactly what Mallis wanted—blood. And plenty of it.

I think Cody could tell that I was reaching a breaking point. He leaned in and placed a hand on my knee. "Do you really think this is something we should try?" I nodded, not trusting myself to speak. "Should we at least get some backup?"

"Who, Cody? The cops? Kendra, assuming she is healed enough? My aunts? The longer we wait for someone to come help us, the more danger we are in of things getting out of control. I just…I just want this over. I want my old life back." I realized how entitled and petulant that sounded, but thankfully Cody let it slip.

"Weapons?"

"We are weapons. Besides, I don't think they would like it too much if we rolled in there with your guns and my silver stakes. No, we give this a try the old-fashioned way."

He shifted in his seat, clearly uncomfortable with that thought. Maybe I was wrong to have told him. I should have done this on my own. Here I was, risking another life again, and this time it was the first—and maybe the last—person I will ever love.

"Okay then."

"Okay?" I asked, unsure of his meaning.

"Yes. If this is the plan, then we do it. I don't like the idea of going in unarmed, but if that's what you think we need to do, then so be it. But one thing: how do we find them?"

Now I brightened up. "I've been thinking about that.

Remember all the times that we've run into the Order or one of their wolves? It's always when they come sniffing around after a magical signature. Hope's house, the coffee shop, Dr. Garner's...hell, even the Shifter encampment." He was nodding, encouraging me to continue. "We know they are recruiting, looking for magic, Shifters, or both. We can use that to our advantage."

"You mean set a lure? Get one of them to come to us?"

"Not quite. I'm more focused on how they are finding us. I started wondering how they are doing it; then I asked myself how I would do it. I'd use a locator spell. It's a beacon that looks for specific signatures, or magical scents, if you will."

"I get it. So they are waiting for something to set off their tracker and then they just follow it to the source?"

"Exactly. We can do the same thing, only in reverse. To cast a specific spell like the ones they use requires considerable power. That kind of power leaves its own signature. If I can find that signature, we can follow it back to the source. And I'm betting that source is the Warlock and whatever witch he has locked up, draining to use as a mystic battery."

"And wherever the Warlock is...the big daddy vamp can't be too far behind!"

I shook my head in distaste. "Uh-uh. Please don't ever use that term again. That was...so bad."

Cody laughed before adding, "So when do we do this?"

"No time like the present. All I need is my trusty crystal ball."

"What? Are you serious? A crystal ball?"

"That muffin wasn't the only reason I wanted to swing by here," I replied. "When I used to do readings for the tourists in town I kept a crystal ball here. Of course, back then it was all for show, but now, with the right magical nudge, it should work just fine as a focal point for a tracking spell."

I got up and walked behind the counter to a small room that served as a combination shop storeroom and office. The tiny space was barely big enough for my desk and chair, let alone the brace of shelving units on the wall that held an array of coffees, my aunts' homemade tea mixtures, and a few other necessary shop products. The shelves also housed my tarot cards (still don't know what the tourists see in those) and a glass ball that I had received as a twelfth birthday present from Aunt Lena. They were just props, of course, but I had a feeling that the crystal ball might be a bit more if I could focus the right spell into it.

I shoved it into my bag and exited the room, returning to Cody's side.

"So, you just going to do it right here?" he asked.

"No. If this works, we need to be ready to move." We placed our coffee cups and the saucer from my muffin on the dirty dish pile behind the counter. I checked to make sure the staff was okay one last time before we made our way out to the car.

I took the crystal ball out and held it on my lap. In the past, when I had used it to enthrall tourists and draw more money out of them, I had pretended to gaze deeply into it, but the truth was I had never really looked into the ball. It was just a ploy, something to augment the card and coffee grounds readings.

But this time was different. I concentrated on the crystal, willing myself to see anything that might exist inside the sphere. I centered my breathing and started whispering to the ball.

The thing about magic is that it's mostly driven by the caster's will. Anyone can learn the incantations, but if the willpower behind the spell is weak, then the outcome will be weak as well. The will powers the spell, so the more willpower a witch possesses, the greater scope she can extend the spell. Add to that the ability to tap into the ambient mystical energies flowing through nature, and you have the rudimentary basics of how magic works.

In my case, I could not only tap into the energy around me, but also into the power that flowed inside my body. I was a Reliquary, and therefore capable of retaining vast amounts of mystic energy. I had expected the energy I had expended throughout the day by raising barriers to have nearly drained my reserves, but that wasn't the case. As I reached deep inside myself, I realized I had plenty of energy left. If anything, I was starting to think that the more I used my magic, the deeper my reserves grew.

I had also been spending a lot of my free time in my aunts' study, memorizing spell after spell in their vast library of mystic tomes. Not only had I memorized the spells, but I had also started to experiment with mixing certain incantations to create new spells...some of which I hoped I would never have to use.

I snapped myself out of my reverie and focused on the task at hand. I needed to find the magical footprint that the Warlock was using to find supernatural and mystical trails. Shouldn't be hard—after all, I had basically done the same thing to create the map Cody and I used. Only this time, I was looking for something a little more specific; a little more malefic, to be exact.

I reached in deep with my mind, willing magic to flow into the glass. Then, I breathed the ancient words of revelation into it, and asked it to show me what I needed to see. Almost immediately, the space within the ball began to fill with a swirling blue mist. It sparked and flared as if a miniature electrical storm was firing inside the globe I held.

Truth be told, I wasn't sure it would work. Or maybe it would only work if the Warlock was actively targeting a mystical source. I waited, practically holding my breath, but nothing happened.

Then I decided to try something just a little different. I concentrated on the memory of Dr. Garner's house the night Cody and I had been attacked—the night that the elder Dr. Garner had been killed. That house had been covered in wards, so that meant someone had actively set them. Wards like that had a lasting signature. I was willing to bet that whoever set them had forgotten to un-make them after the house burnt down—why would they remember?

I was surprised when I suddenly sensed a ping. The trace magic from the wards was indeed still there, and stronger than I had expected. I could feel the swirl inside the ball latching onto the signature.

"Yes, that's it," I whispered. "Now find it!"

Instantly, the light within the crystal ball flared out, filling the car with luminescence. I was nearly blinded by the suddenness of it, and through squinted eyes I could see the eerie bluish light taking the form of a large hawk, its wings and feathers alight with blue fire. It shot out of the car, passing through the windshield before rocketing out of the parking lot and streaking down the road.

"Cody! Follow it!"

"What? Follow what, Allie? What just happened?"

Fuck! He couldn't see eldritch energy, at least not the way I could.

"Out of the parking lot and turn left! Just go!"

Cody peeled out of the lot, nearly sideswiping a

Cherokee in the process, but then proceeded to haul ass down Route 15, following my directions. The hawk was flying down the road. It stayed only a few feet above the road, passing through any cars or trucks that it approached in a phantom-ghost-hawk kind of way. I could still make out the fading light it left behind as it streaked toward the city.

Queen City was roughly ten miles outside of Trinity Cove. Technically, we were a suburb of the city, but it didn't feel like it. Our little community was tucked away, and had yet to be discovered by the baby-stroller-slash-hipster-wannabe crowd. This was partly because other than my coffee shop, there was not a lot to appeal to that crowd, but also I was beginning to think that there might be something else keeping the city-dwellers at bay: the same energy that flowed through the ley lines around Trinity Cove and attracted supernaturals also acted as a natural repellent against most normal humans. Something in the back of their minds, something left over from the time when all humans had reason to fear the dark, told them this was not the best place to raise a family.

The good thing was that it went both ways: most of the people that lived in the Cove rarely ventured into the city. There was nothing it offered that we couldn't get in Trinity —and at a much reduced price. Still, both places relied on tourists' dollars to help support growth and keep the municipal coffers filled, so what happened to one would eventually affect the other. I didn't want to think what a Trinity overcome with monsters and vampires would mean for Queen City. But I also had no intention of anyone finding out the answer to that. I pushed the thought away as I directed Cody onto, and then off of, the freeway that led into the city proper.

"Makes sense," Cody said. "These roads lead to the

warehouse district of the city. No better place for a vamp lair than out here—mostly deserted buildings and no residential construction."

He was right. We crossed over a set of train tracks and found ourselves driving by one derelict building after another. Broken windows and boarded-up doors adorned most of the now defunct factories that made up the old shipping districts. Ahead of us, I saw my conjured spirit guide rise up in the air, circling a two-story building that squatted before us.

Anything to keep the sun out, I realized.

The hawk circled the building a few times before diving dramatically into the structure, passing harmlessly through the roof.

"That's it." I pointed. "That's where the energy source is located."

"Great," said Cody, easing off the road and coming to a stop behind a stand of trees. "That definitely looks like a lair for a nasty Daddy Va..." He caught himself, even before my eyes could cut into him. "You sure we want to go in there? Just the two of us?"

"No," I answered truthfully, "but I also don't think we have a choice. I've had enough of this fighting; let's see what these bitches want."

I took off my jean jacket, drew my hair up into a high ponytail, and summoned my courage. Taking a deep breath together, we headed for the warehouse, and whoever—or whatever—might be waiting inside.

Chapter Twelve

"Remember," I said, "we are not here to fight with wolves. Recon only: we get in, get some info, and get out." I had reluctantly agreed that maybe we make this first trip a recon mission. Get the lay of our enemies' whereabouts and gather some intel. Then, once we knew that this was indeed where Mallis was, maybe we could come back and chat with them.

"You make that sound so easy." Cody's tone was tense and hard to read. He was focused on the task at hand, however, and that was what really mattered.

"Okay. I've done what I can to get us this far. Now it's your turn."

He nodded and instantly began to shift into his hybrid form. As soon as he transformed, I placed a containment spell around him. It would allow him to fully experience the world around us while masking his nature as a Shifter from both magical and enhanced physical senses. I needed for him to be able to track Shira, but didn't want to set off any alarms that we were about to enter the building.

We made our way to one of the loading docks along the back of the building. I gently probed for wards, but found none. The Warlock was too cocky to set any, or he didn't want to waste precious energy from whatever source he was draining. Either way, it was good for us. If there were no magical defenses, that meant there were probably physical ones in the form of wolves or other Shifters that may have been recruited by this point. Isn't that how the Warlock had used Shifters before being banished by my mother? They acted as their daytime guardians.

And now daylight guardians would be all the more important, since the Warlock was possibly in league with vampires. This was the one reason I didn't want to wait for the cover of darkness, the other being that if we needed to make a hasty retreat, at least Mallis wouldn't follow us outside. No, sneaking into a potential vamp nest at night was not high on my bucket list.

We approached the door and I gave the handle a quick tug to see if it would open. The building may have been rundown and derelict, but the doors were all new, with solid pull-bars for handles and no discernible locking mechanism. The door didn't budge.

"Maybe I can force it open," growled Cody, stepping forward.

"No. Too noisy and threatening. Let me try." I placed my hand on the latch and willed my magic to flow into it, filling the tiny crevices and tumblers that comprised the hidden locking mechanism. I filled the space with power that covered all of the little nooks and crannies, and then pushed on the door. It slid open effortlessly, and more important, silently. Immediately I extended the shield I had created around Cody to cover both of us. I had no idea what a witch smells like to these Shifters, but I wasn't taking any chances.

We pressed ourselves against the inside of the wall as soon as we were through the door. When we eased it shut behind us, we were cast into darkness as all of the windows, over a full story above us, were neatly boarded up.

"Can you hear anything?" I asked Cody.

He cocked his head to one side, eyes closed. "Yes. Ahead of us, there's a bunch of rooms splintering off from a larger gathering area. There's definitely something going on in the bigger one. I can make out muffled voices and…I can smell fear in the air."

"Any other wolves?"

He shook his head. "Not sure. There are so many scents here, including ones I can't make heads or tails of."

Made sense. Could be other Shifters he had never encountered, or some other supernaturals we had yet to meet. Either way, caution was the name of the game as we made our way forward. I had to rely on Cody to guide us in the near blackness because I didn't want to risk the glow of my magic giving us away. He led and I followed, my hand grasped lightly in his. I resisted the urge to run my thumb back and forth across his hand, marveling in the feel of his silky smooth fur.

Halfway up the corridor, we could see the tiniest bit of light leaking into the hall from the room ahead. I could also hear human voices, faint at first but gaining in clarity the closer we crept. Cody stopped, his spine rigid, as he tilted his head back slightly to sniff the air. He quickly pulled at my hand and we sprinted for the cover of shadows, pressing our backs into a corner underneath a stairwell to our left. No sooner had we flattened ourselves into the shadows than two men walked out of the lit room and down the hallway.

They were grumbling to one another under their breath as one lit a cigarette and passed the lighter to his friend.

I couldn't make out what they were complaining about, but even in the fading light I had no trouble spotting the dark glint of a rifle slung over each man's arm. Guards. Human guards.

Cody glanced at me, and I could practically read his thoughts. I nodded in agreement: it was way too risky to try getting any closer. He nodded at the staircase above us and a lightbulb went off in both of our minds simultaneously. He gathered my hand in his and led us up the staircase to a loft area. Musty boxes and crates strewn about told me that the space had been used as storage during the warehouse productivity days. We picked our way around stacked crates and moldy boxes until we came to the edge of the loft, where an iron-spindled guardrail allowed an overlook into the cavernous space below.

We dropped to our stomachs and inched far enough forward that we could see between the rails into the room below, where the voices had originated. The room was solid concrete and devoid of any furniture. A couple of naked overhead light bulbs dangling from the ceiling high above was the only source of light in the space. The walls of the room were lined with all kinds of guns, arranged in neat rows covering nearly every square inch of the room. It reminded me a little of that scene in The Matrix when Keanu told the Operator they needed "guns...lots of guns." Two men with iPads were walking around the room, making notations as they went.

"...why we get stuck doing this shit while everyone else is out having fun collecting the freaks," came one gruff voice.

"Someone has to inventory everything and make sure

we have enough of the right kinds of ammo for all these," came an equally gruff reply.

"I know," acknowledged Good Number One. "But last night we drew guard duty and had to stay outside the whole fucking evening. I'm getting a little stir-crazy, and itchy to get out in the field again."

"I hear that. But you heard The Man. Hs said we all have to do our part, and when the time comes, there will be plenty of action to go around."

Goon Number One mumbled something in response that I couldn't hear, but it elicited a laugh out of Goon Number Two. "Yeah, that was fun. I still don't see why we had to shoot that cat-lady. She would have made a nice addition to the ranks."

Jesus. They were talking about Kendra. I could feel Cody bristling next to me, and I had to give his hand a squeeze to calm him.

"I know. But like The Man said, some of them would be too hard to turn. Plus, she was better off being used to send that bitch a message."

What were they talking about? What did they mean by "turned"? And...was I the "bitch" they were talking about?

I felt Cody tap me on the shoulder. He nodded his head toward a small catwalk that led away from the overlook. We inched our way backward until we were safely out of their view, before we stood up and headed down the walkway to another section of the warehouse. It became clear that there was an interconnecting series of walkways that led to various storage lofts overlooking holding bins, like the ones where Goons One and Two had been stationed.

Most of the rooms were empty, with a couple containing wooden boxes stacked neatly throughout them.

"This is turning out to be a bust," said Cody in low, coarse whisper.

"Maybe we should make our way back to the thugs in the armory. We can take the two of them. We could grab one and force him to tell us what the hell is going on."

Before he could respond, Cody stiffened once again. I could practically feel the hair on his back beginning to rise, and a low rumble gathering in his chest.

"Cody, what is it?"

He raised a finger to his lips and led me across the final catwalk toward another room at the back of the warehouse, a soft glow emanating from within. As we got closer, I could hear a voice speaking. I may not have been covered in fur like Cody, but nevertheless I felt my hackles rise. I knew that raspy voice. It belonged to the Warlock.

A blast of cold gripped me as I instantly broke out in a cold sweat. I followed Cody to the edge of the loft space and peered over the railing. This room was completely different from the others. It was not a containment space, holding weapons or God knows what else; no, this one looked like living quarters. The cold, concrete floor was covered by a plush ornamental rug that stretched nearly wall to wall. There was an arrangement of weathered leather chairs and a sprawling couch surrounding a mahogany coffee table. Floor lamps provided comfortable lighting for the space, illuminating bookshelves that were crammed almost as full as my aunts'.

The room itself was larger than the others. It occupied not only the space we could see, but it also continued under the loft on which we crouched. A shadowy figure stepped into the center of the room, cloaked in a black, hooded robe. I caught my breath and drew my shields closer around us as the Warlock turned to address someone outside of our field of view—someone that was in the area under the loft, directly below us.

"I don't know how much longer she'll last," said the Warlock. "She is nearly drained. I can power a few more locators out of her, probably siphon enough energy to do another divination if need be, but after that she will not be of much use."

"Then we need to find another," came a voice from beneath us. It was calm and deep, masculine, and carried just the right amount of authority so as not to leave any doubt as to who was in charge. "We are so close."

"Yes we are. But there is a problem: I have studied the ancient runes you shared, and I am not certain the spell can be cast with just one witch tethered to it. We will need more power, more witches. Once the spell starts, it would be disastrous if we could not summon enough power to complete it."

"Yes, so I have heard. What about the other source?"

"That is...untested. We have no idea if it would actually work."

What other source was he talking about? I turned to Cody to see if maybe he had an inclination as to what they were talking about. He just shook his head and shrugged.

"Can you get a read on who the Warlock is talking to?" I whispered.

Before he could answer, a low, threatening growl greeted us. It came from behind us and we both turned just in time to see a large wolf emerge from the shadows. How the hell had one managed to get this close to us without tripping my magic or Cody's senses? The wolf charged, and as it barrelled toward us out of the darkness I suddenly recognized her.

Shira.

Chapter Thirteen

When Shira hit us, it felt like being run over by a train. Well, at least how I imagine it would feel. She had sprinted across the few feet that separated us before I could expand my shields and ran headfirst into both me and Cody. The impact knocked the breath out of me and elicited a roar of pain from Cody.

We struck the railing, and together, the three of us toppled up and over, out into space. I instinctively drew my shield around myself as I realized I was falling; still, the crash onto the hard concrete ten feet below knocked all of the breath from my lungs. I closed my eyes against the sudden flash of stars that danced in my mind's eye. I heard Cody grunt in pain as he landed awkwardly next to me. Only Shira was silent as she landed on all fours like a cat, completely comfortable in her wolf form.

I rolled to one side just in time to see Cody get to his feet, right in front of Shira. In a blur, she shifted to her hybrid, half-human half-wolf form and lunged forward, driving her fist into his midsection and sending him flying against the far wall. I tried to blink away the silver dots that were floating in my vision long enough to summon a blast of magic and hurl it in Shira's direction.

The wolf never turned to face me, but instead leapt up and backward in a graceful display of athleticism. She somersaulted backward over my blast, and it struck the floor where she had been standing. In midair, as her powerful body flipped and rotated in my direction, she shifted fully into her wolf form again, landing on all-fours facing me. She charged, moving so fast that I couldn't draw a bead on her.

She launched at me, and I instinctively rolled a shield in place to take the brunt of the impact. I channeled blue force into my fists and struck her with an uppercut that slammed her jaws shut. Without missing a beat, she rolled with the punch, shifting again into her hybrid form. She pivoted, bringing her leg up and around in a vicious kick, her heel slamming into my midsection. I felt all the air leave me as I rocketed backward, slamming into, then over, the large coffee table behind me.

Before I could regain any sense of balance, she was on me again, this time in full wolf form. The sheer weight of her body pressing down on me prevented my already burning lungs from drawing a breath. She was determined to cave in my chest, through cartilage and bone to the vital bits beneath. I was certain I would hear a pop at any second as my brittle bones gave in to the pressure. She leaned forward, her razor sharp canines aiming for my jugular.

Her jaws snapped shut so close to my face that I felt the spray of saliva fly from them. And then, she suddenly yelped in pain. She whirled her head around to confront Cody, who was in full wolf form, and had clamped his jaws onto her hindquarters so hard that I could see blood seeping from them. I used the distraction to place my hand in front of Shira's face, and fired off a burst of strobe light magic. It flared bright as sunlight in her eyes, and immediately threw her off guard. At the same time I brought my knee up, catching her in her soft underbelly. She roared in pain and confusion, allowing Cody to dig in deeper, and with a heave of his upper body he was able to throw Shira off of me.

She hit the floor with a thud, and instantly Cody was on her. Again she shifted, ignoring the blood running from her side. Her change in form allowed her to slip under and away from Cody, and before he could react she swept him up in a powerful grip and threw his bulk effortlessly at me. I dropped the shimmering blast of magic I was readying so as not to hurt Cody, leaving me completely unprepared for the impact with his enormous body. Luckily, he had twisted in midair at the last moment, trying to evade a full collision with me. It worked; I was struck only by his flank in passing. Still, it was enough to once again send me crashing through more furniture.

This time I could feel myself easing in and out of consciousness. I was aware of Cody's howls of pain as Shira again pounced on him, but he sounded so far away…his sharp yelps in the rolling darkness were like pinpricks against my skin. I was on my back, and every fiber of my being cried out in pain as I tried to make sense of what was happening. The feeling of nausea threatened to overcome me as I tried to roll onto my side. Just then, I felt myself being yanked forward. Someone…or something was dragging me by one leg across the floor.

I lifted my head and looked down my body. Through blurry vision I made out Shira's furry, hybrid form. She had one hand clamped around my ankle in a vice-like grip that I was afraid would crush bones. She looked back at me, bared her fangs and growled threateningly, just before stopping and releasing my leg.

My head throbbed as I tried to focus on the voices that were filtering through the fog around me. I could tell I wasn't in the same room where we had fought, but I had no idea where she had taken me. How long had I been out?

"...should kill her now, before she can cause us any more trouble." It was the ragged voice of the Warlock cutting through my haze.

"Gladly," came Shira's guttural reply. Before I realized it, she was once again on top of me. She lifted my head off the ground and turned it to one side, exposing my neck. I saw her draw back her other hand, fingers stiffened with those impossibly long, dagger-like claws extended, that she was preparing to drive through skin, muscle and bone. I closed my eyes as I sensed the death blow coming.

"Stop!" said a single voice, halting Shira's arm in mid-strike. "Shira, heel."

Incredibly, she shifted to her wolf form and trotted away from me without so much as a look back. I drew myself to a sitting position, first looking around for Cody, who I couldn't see, and then toward Shira.

The she-wolf had stepped up onto a raised platform that was illuminated by another overhead light fixture. The only piece of furniture present was a single high-backed leather chair. A lone figure sat on the chair, and reached out to slowly stroke the hair of the werewolf. She growled low in her chest, but it didn't sound like the same threatening timbre that I was accustomed to hearing. It almost sounded pleasurable...the canine version of a contented cat's purr. I tried to focus on the figure's face, but the odd shadows kept it hidden.

"So," came a masculine voice, "you are the current Reliquary. I must say, I expected more from such a renowned race of witches."

I raised a hand to my eyes, trying to shield them from the light. "Who are you? And where is Cody?"

"Oh, I wouldn't worry about that mongrel, little girl. And you know who I am."

He gave Shira one last appreciative ruffle across her massive head, then stood up. He was tall, nearly six and a half feet, but thin. He was dressed in dark denim jeans and a green long-sleeved crew-neck shirt, with a red dragon emblazoned across the front. He stepped off the platform without making a sound, and walked over to me. His steps were long and fluid, his arms clasped behind his back. As he came closer I could make out his pale features. A sharp, birdlike face was highlighted by a prominent Roman nose and jet-black eyes. His hair was long, but swept up into one of those hipster man-buns that I hated so much. He leaned forward and smiled in my face. His tongue darted out and ran smoothly over two pronounced, long incisors. I recoiled in horror at the rotten smell that emanated from his mouth as his eyes squinted at me in glee.

"Mallis," I breathed.

Chapter Fourteen

The fact that I had said his name aloud brought him a chuckle. He threw his head back and laughed, but at what, I hadn't the foggiest idea. I thought maybe it was one of those stereotypical things the bad guys did in movies to show their enjoyment at making some innocent victim squirm. But this wasn't make-believe or a bad SyFy movie. His pasty skin wasn't the result of improperly applied makeup, and those teeth sure as shit weren't prosthetics.

"I know you too, Allison Caine," he said, turning his back to me to take his seat once again.

"Where's Cody?" I asked again, trying to control the tremble in my voice.

"Well, he's not dead, if that's what you're asking."

It wasn't, but knowing that helped me to breathe a little easier. My head was still ringing from the beat-down Shira had laid on me, but I tried to push that pain aside and reach for my magic. "We didn't come here to fight." I tried to stall; I just needed my head to clear a little longer so I could focus.

"No? So, what exactly did you come here for?" he asked. He cocked his head to one side, seemingly genuinely interested in my answer.

"Recon. Your goons have been raiding the encampment of residents of Trinity Cove. You've killed people close to me, and have been bragging about starting a war in my town. I wanted to see if there was any way to find out what was really going on."

"You could have asked, you know." I didn't know what to say. I wasn't expecting such nonchalance. "I mean, it's not like I really have anything to worry about from you. If you wanted to know what I was up to, you should have asked."

Okay. I'll play along. I could feel the thrum of my magic start to replace the pounding inside my skull. "You want to bring about the Leveling, right? To blot out the sun?"

He didn't bother to hide his shock before an ear-to-ear grin split his face. "You surprise me, Miss Caine. You know more than I expected. Yes; I want the freedom to walk the earth anytime I please, night or day."

"You do know it's a myth, don't you? The Leveling isn't possible. It's on old vamp's tale."

"Well, now that's where you're wrong. Tell me, what do you know about me?" He sat back in his chair and crossed his legs.

"I know that you are the oldest vampire on record to have migrated to the new world…"

"One of the oldest," he interrupted, "but do continue."

I filed that bit of information away for later. "I know that even for a vampire as old as you are, you still have vulnerability to the sun." I hesitated, focusing on my magic, wondering how much I could summon. Would be enough to at least take him down long enough for me to run?

"And?" he offered. "Please, continue." I just stared at him, narrowing my eyes. "That's it? That's the sum knowledge you possess of me? Rule one of battle, little girl: know thine enemy. After all, I made it a point to know you."

He hesitated, waiting to see what effect his words might have on me. When I didn't respond, he continued, his voice a little too cheery for my liking. "I know that you're the eldest of two, younger brother Garland...oh, has he come out of the closet to you yet? Never mind, not important. I know that you and your brother were raised by your two aunts, who are also witches, Lena and Vivian. I believe they are Elemental witches, am I correct? Unlike you, who was born a Reliquary. I know that you weren't officially trained in the craft, that you pretty much just tinkered with your art until recently, when it started to bloom. I know that you think you're in love with a werewolf, and that he is definitely in love with you. I know that you outgrew your fear of thinking something was always hiding in your closet at night, but now that you've seen what really does go bump in the night, your old fears have returned. You can't fall asleep anymore if your closet door is slightly ajar...even though there's a big bad wolf curled up right next to you." He paused, licking his lips obscenely at me and probing me with those dark eyes.

I had to admit, he was getting to me. How the hell did he know all of that? But he wasn't scaring me; he was pissing the shit out of me. *Just keep talking...I have something very special for you.*

"Tell me, does the new town vet know that you were with her aunt when she died? Does she know that you were the one who burned that house down? Does she know that you couldn't save her aunt? Probably not. But then again, you have never been very good at saving people, have you?

At least your mother had that going for her. Now, that was a witch that knew how to get things done."

I froze, ice running through my veins. "What did you just say, monster?"

He looked around as if he had to double-check where the question came from, then he spun to face me again. "I said, your mother knew how to get things done. She was something else, that one. Maybe, if you were a fraction of the witch she was, you wouldn't be so…ineffectual."

That was it. My mind exploded in fire and I screamed with all my strength, pouring my hatred and anger into a single bolt of pure magic that would liquefy that bastard on the spot. I leaned forward and raised both hands, sending the magic pouring toward my target. I summoned elemental magic and let loose twin bolts of power that…did nothing.

It wasn't like the magic didn't hit him; it was more like the magic just…didn't. It didn't manifest. Nothing came erupting out of me. Not even a spark. To anyone watching, I must have looked like a crazy woman, waving her hands in front of her face and screaming.

Mallis looked at me, blinking, his mouth agape in a mock look of terror. "Oh wow. I'm sure whatever that was meant to be it would have been quite…impressive." Again, he strolled over to the chair and took a seat facing me.

"What have you done to me?" I managed to say as I looked down at my hands. I could feel the magic inside me…it was definitely there, but it wasn't manifesting the way I commanded it to.

"Oh, I haven't done anything to you. It's the room." He gestured around the space with both hands. "It's what you might call a magical leaching space. It is keyed on witchcraft; it drains mystical energy and stores it…elsewhere, for my followers to draw upon as needed. So whatever you just did was taken and stored in a central battery, if you will. And judging from the near orgasmic look on my ward's face, whatever you just unleashed must have been a doozy."

I glanced around the room, landing on the Warlock, who stood immobile, face tilted up to the ceiling. When he lowered his head, I could see his features were slack, his eyes rolled back in his head, so that all that was visible was the quivering white of his eyes. His breathing was even more ragged than usual as he spoke to Mallis.

"By the Seven, my liege...her power...so raw, so... untapped."

"Did you get what you needed?" Mallis said.

"Yes. And then some. We must drain her!" the Warlock said, focusing his gaze on me as he stepped forward.

"Not yet," said Mallis, his voice stopping the Warlock in his tracks. Well, his voice and the warning growl that emanated from Shira. "We may yet have need of her."

I dropped my hands into my lap. I felt hollowed...both magically and emotionally. "Whatever. Kill me, drain me... I obviously can't stop you. I'll cooperate with whatever it is you have planned; just let my friend go. Please."

Mallis again focused his attention on the Warlock, completely ignoring me now. "Was it there? Does it match the energy signature?"

"Yes," replied the Warlock. "We have the signature."

Mallis sat back in his chair, that evil grin once again staining his face as he reached out a single hand and languidly stroked Shira. "Thank you, Allie. We couldn't have done this without you."

Now I was angry, and on guard. "What are you talking about? I would never help you."

"Not willingly, no," Mallis replied. "But you have proven incredibly easy to manipulate. I wonder why that is?"

"What are you talking about?" I repeated.

"We have the map from your friend," Mallis said. "The one showing us where the supernaturals are hiding in your little community."

I could feel a chill crawl up my spine. Cody would have never given that map up, not while he was still breathing.

Mallis waved his hand dismissively in my direction. "Don't worry. Your pet isn't dead."

I swallowed hard. Maybe it was true what they said about vampires being able to read minds.

"Personally I would have killed him, but my ward here wants to keep him, see if he can be reacclimated into the fold."

"Let me guess," I said, "you were the one that was behind the message that went out to the parents of the wolves, to convince them to bring their children back to Trinity Cove."

"Of course. How else would we have found them? Of course, not all of them have shown up just yet, but that's okay. And some have never really left Trinity at all, just been in deep cover. Kind of like your friend Cody." He stood up and walked toward me again, his hands clasped behind his back. "He will be instrumental in bringing the others to my side."

"Cody will never help you!"

"Just like you didn't? We'll see."

"It doesn't matter if you have the map or not. Trinity Cove and the surrounding area cover a lot of land. Word will spread that you're looking for supernaturals long before you stumble across one."

"See, now that's what I thought," said Mallis, turning away from me, "but that's where you came into the picture. The ley lines that flow through Trinity block my Warlock's power; as talented as he may be, he could never have cast a revelation spell to show us where the witches are. But you..." Again he smiled, licking his lips. "It only took the slightest of prods to get you to cast your shielding spells—spells that are surrounding each and every home of someone we might be interested in. All we needed to find those shields was a sample of your power signature, which you so graciously just provided. You marked our targets for us."

I swallowed hard, my head starting to spin again. "Good luck getting through those shields." I hoped I sounded more positive than I felt.

Mallis again waved his hand contemptuously. "Oh, we don't need luck. Here's the thing about magical barriers: they work against the supernatural just fine. But they aren't so effective against a human that just walks up and...oh, I don't know...kicks in a door."

Jesus. What had I done?

"What do you want with them? Whatever you're after, I'm sure they have nothing to do with it," I manage.

"So you would think. But the fact of the matter is, after over a millennium walking this earth, I long for the old days —the days when humans knew they were prey and respected the food chain. Now, we, the ones who sit at the top of that chain, are relegated to children's scary bedtime stories and figments of tired imaginations. We are cartooned and lampooned as things that simply...sparkle."

He whirled to look at me, his face a mask of anger and disgust, his dark eyes now glowing like red coals. "Well, enough is enough. It's time to remind those meatbags out there just why they used to fear the night so much. Only this time, that fear will creep into their daylight waking hours as well. Because once the Leveling is upon them, they will be fair game any hour of the day, ripe for the picking whenever my appetite rises.

"As for the Shifters...I need to restore balance. Long ago, when the Shifters aligned themselves with the witches, they sent a message to me, one that said they would rather stand with humans than with their supernatural brothers and sisters. Well, I intend to answer that message with bloodshed. Either they stand with us...or they will no longer stand. Humanity's reign is coming to an end, my dear."

"You are batshit crazy," was all I could muster. "The Leveling isn't possible. All you're going to do is get a lot of people—human and supernatural alike—killed. And for what? An age-old fairy tale."

He laughed, throwing his head back maniacally. "See, that's where you're wrong, my dear. It is real. I've seen it! And I will not rest until I bring it back...only this time, it will be permanent. It's too bad your mother's shade is gone. You could ask her; she knew it was real. Why do you think she volunteered to spend what would have been an eternity maintaining a forbidding? It wasn't to keep my young ward at bay. She knew what my minions were, and the forbidding she created was designed with one purpose only: to stop the Leveling. But now...thanks to you, that is one more thing we don't have to worry about."

At that moment, I felt everything rush out of me. I felt deflated and beaten. Hot tears welled behind my eyes and I let my chin drop to my chest before that monster could see them.

And that was when the room was suddenly swallowed by the eruptions of gunfire, the screams of dying men and a deafening roar of an animal too large to be found in nature.

Chapter Fifteen

I wasn't the only one caught off-guard by the screams. Mallis looked around in bewilderment, and the Warlock finally snapped out of his magic-induced rapture. Even Shira seemed caught unaware as she leapt off the platform where she had been resting, shifting to her more flexible hybrid form.

"What was that?" yelled Mallis at no one in particular.

More explosions followed. This time, they were actual explosions, the kind that rang my ears; they were close. I glanced at Shira and could see the wolf shaking her head to clear her ears of the concussive blasts. I took full advantage of the distraction, and dragged myself to my feet as I searched for a way out. The door to the room was only about fifteen feet away, but another series of explosions nearly knocked me off my feet before I could make for the exit.

Out of the corner of my eye, I saw the Warlock begin to move toward me, only to be intercepted by Mallis. The vampire hastily whispered into his ear, and a second later, the Warlock vanished toward the back of the room, disappearing into the darkness of the corners. Again, I staggered toward the door, this time met by a roar that stopped me cold. It didn't come from behind me, so I knew it wasn't Shira threatening me; rather it emanated from just outside.

Before I could run through the doorway, an enormous lion pushed its way into the space. It was easily twelve hundred pounds and stood close to seven feet in height. Its massive head was surrounded by a majestic, golden mane that was splattered with blood and gore. The beast roared upon entering the room, and I could have sworn the walls shook in response. But as surprising as was the sight of a giant lion stepping into the room, it paled in comparison to what followed behind.

Esmay leapt through the opening, her rapier glinting and covered in a dark, viscous fluid. She held it before her as she charged into the space, her beautiful features a mask of fury and damnation, her hair pulled back in her signature high ponytail, highlighting the dark streaks of blood smearing her face.

"Esmay...what are you—" I began, but was quickly cut off by two men that followed her into the room, brandishing what looked like automatic rifles.

One of the men was instantly swept up by the lion. I could hear the sickening crunch of bone as his spine was snapped in a single bite from the great beast. The second man, momentarily distracted by the grisly fate of his comrade, fell to the end of Esmay's rapier as she danced around behind him in a blur of fluid movements, slashing at his back and finally impaling him. He dropped silently to the floor, never having the chance to squeeze off a single round from his weapon.

"C'mon!" Esmay screamed at me. "We don't have long

before reinforcements arrive!" She reached into her jacket pocket and withdrew a tiny black cylinder device with a button on top of it. She depressed the switch and threw it toward still-confused Shira and Mallis.

Instinctively, I followed her as she dived out the door. I was vaguely aware of the lion moving his large body to shield us from the blast of the concussion grenade that rocked the room. I could hear Shira howl in response, but I couldn't tell if it was out of pain or anger.

I shook my head to clear my ears, and when I looked up I could see Esmay sprinting down the hallway. I followed, still a little uneasy on my feet, but I managed to keep up nonetheless.

"Wait," I shouted after her, "we have to find Cody!"

"It's okay," she called back. "He's taken care of!"

The farther we got away from that room, the better I felt. Whatever that place was made of, it seriously fucked with my mojo—but I could feel my head clearing almost immediately. We sprinted down the warehouse corridor toward what I assumed was an exit. We passed several smaller rooms, one of which garnered my attention.

It felt like a tug at the back of my mind that was impossible to ignore. I stopped, breathing hard, and looked in through the small window in the center of the locked steel door.

"What is it?" Esmay breathed as she ran back to my side.

"Not sure. Something...is in there. Something that doesn't belong here."

The room beyond the window was bathed in darkness, and I couldn't make out any shapes or movement. I put my ear to the door, listening for any signs of life. What I wouldn't give for wolf hearing right about now.

Esmay tugged at my elbow. "Allie, come on…we need to get out of here."

Then I felt it. The slightest of touches brushed my mind, like a whisper in my ear.

Magic.

But so…weak. A candle that had burned down to little more than a puddle of wax—one that wouldn't flicker much longer.

There was a captive witch in there.

Anger welled up inside me, and I channeled magic into my hand. I focused on the door, trying to force it open. Counter-resistance crept from the cold metal—the door had been sealed with a mystical ward, one that was repelling my magic. I could feel my brow furrow as I dug deeper, pitting more and more of my magic against the counter-spell.

"Allie!" Esmay shouted, pointing behind us.

Turning around, I could see Shira was charging down the hall, heading right for us. I swung my hand up, throwing a bolt of magic at the wolf. Out of the corner of my eye I could see Esmay mirroring my movement, and I looked to the side just enough to see that she also threw something at the werewolf. It was black and shiny, with a tiny red light blinking as it flew end over end down the hall.

Stun grenade, I assumed—the same one that had been used back in the room. Shira skidded to a stop, shifting to her more nimble hybrid form and leaping to one side of the hallway just as the grenade went off with a sickening boom. The hall rocked, and thick smoke poured from the projectile.

"That won't stop them for long!" cried Esmay.

I turned to the steel door, knowing I wouldn't have time to get it open. I placed my head briefly against the window and closed my eyes.

I'll be back for you. I promise.

The barest whisper of a reply grazed my mind, and then, at Esmay's urging, I was off and running again. Somewhere behind me I heard a lion roar, followed by gunfire and more explosions. I thought briefly that we should go back and help, but Esmay must have sensed my hesitation. She nodded for me to hurry as we approached the doors that led to the loading docks. Sunlight streamed in through the cracks in the board-covered windows. It seemed so long ago that Cody and I had first made our way into the building; I had forgotten it was still daylight.

My lungs and my legs were burning when we finally made it outside. We kept running until we were about a hundred feet away from the building, and then we turned to face it. I was doubled over, hands on my knees, gulping air. I looked over at Esmay and noted that she was hardly even sweating, let alone breathing hard.

"Where…what about Cody?" I asked.

She pointed at the building. "There. Third floor window!"

I looked up, shading my eyes from the sun. There were sections of windows across the entire backside of the warehouse. These, too, were covered in sheets of plywood to keep out the sunlight. Before I could ask her what I was looking for, one group of the windows exploded outward in a storm of debris.

I instinctively stepped back as the large frame of a lion filled the air, effortlessly making the 30-foot drop to the ground. At his side was a smaller, but just as majestic, black panther.

Kendra.

My heart leapt as they approached. Only when they were closer could I make out a human form draped across the lion's back, holding onto its mane. It was Cody, bleeding and weak, as he struggled to maintain his grip on the large Shifter.

"Look out!" cried Esmay.

I looked up in time to see the glint of sunlight reflecting off of two gun barrels, pointed down at us from the shattered window. Throwing up my arms, I managed to erect a shield just as a hail of bullets rained down on us. I stepped forward, lowering my arms and then thrusting them forward, commanding a wave of magic to spider off the shield and slam upward into the windows, cutting through the men holding their rifles. Then, I took things a step further, and—I split those tendrils of power into countless other stabbing arms, and threw them against all of the boarded-up windows I could see.

They punched through glass and splintered wood, leaving the entire backside of the warehouse exposed to the sun. It wouldn't do much damage to the Warlock and Shira, but hopefully it would keep Mallis busy re-fortifying his stronghold, and prevent him from coming after us as soon as night fell.

I ran over to Cody's side to check him. He was barely conscious and bleeding heavily from his arms, back and sides.

"What the hell did they do to him?" I asked no one in particular.

"He will heal," said Esmay. "We need to get him back to the clinic where Isla can patch him up. We have a truck parked a couple of blocks away."

"Thank you," I said, placing a hand on Esmay's arm. "How did you know?"

"Those two." She nodded at Kendra and the lion. "Your boyfriend sent a message to her phone, explaining what you two were up to. He told her if he didn't text by a certain time to bring the cavalry. It's a good thing he did that." She gave me a side-eye that I wasn't sure I could interpret.

"Wait, who is this?" I nodded in the lion's direction.

At that moment, Kendra shifted back to human form and walked over to the golden lion. He knelt down enough that she was able to lift Cody off his back and cradle him in her arms. Then the lion shifted from his enormous, bulky frame to a slender, athletic male form.

"Hey, Allie," said Jhamal.

Chapter Sixteen

I rode in the back of the black Escalade with Cody's head resting in my lap. Esmay drove, while Shira rode shotgun and Jhamal sat in the middle row.

"Are his pupils dilated?" Esmay asked from the front seat. She had called Isla as she drove to tell her we were inbound with a severely injured Cody. Isla had asked what had happened to him, but none of us were able to answer properly since we hadn't actually seen what was done to him.

"No, I don't think so," I yelled. "He's just really cold and clammy. He's bleeding a lot from this wound on his left arm!"

"I'm switching to hands-free," said Esmay. "I can't focus on the road and relay messages at the same time."

Just then, Dr. Garner's voice echoed out of the SUV's speaker system for all to hear. "…with magic?"

"What? I didn't catch that," I replied.

"Can you slow the bleeding with magic?" Isla repeated.

"I already tried that. I can slow it, but as soon as I stop, it starts flowing again. It's like the blood is pumping out or something…"

"Okay, keep pressure on the wound. Esmay, how far out are you, babe?"

"Two minutes. I'll pull into our private parking spot around back. We will come in that way and hopefully not be seen by anyone."

A minute and a half later, the large SUV screeched to a halt behind the veterinary clinic. Dr. Garner was standing at the back door, holding it open.

"Put him in the surgical suite," she said to Kendra, who was carrying Cody into the building.

I tried to follow into the back room, but Isla placed a gentle hand on my shoulder and shook her head. "You know the drill." I backed off and she disappeared down the hall after Kendra.

I went outside, where Esmay was studying the carnage in the back of the truck. It looked like one of Dexter's kill rooms.

"You are really racking up a tab, you know," she said. "Don't think I'm not keeping a running bill for you." I hoped she was joking, but something told me she wasn't.

"Thank you," was all I could say.

"Don't thank me," she replied. "What were you thinking, going off after Mallis alone like that? You're lucky we got there when we did."

I didn't say anything, but instead looked up to see Jhamal walk into the clinic. I followed him to the waiting room, where he was helping himself to a K-cup.

"Hey," I asked. "So, does my brother know you're a Shifter? I mean, is that what you are? Because you don't give off the mystical keynotes of a Shifter."

He shook his head. "No, he doesn't know. And no, I'm not a Shifter...not a true one anyway."

"What are you?"

"I'm a Totem Shifter," Jhamal said.

"What's that?" I asked. "I've never heard of one before."

"I can transform into my inner Totem, or magical self, with the aid of an amulet that has been blessed by a witch, allowing my inner self to run free for a time. But it isn't the same as a Shifter. I can't morph into a hybrid form, or choose to remain in animal form for an indefinite amount of time."

"So on the inside you're a...giant lion?"

He brightened up considerably, quickly nodding his head in agreement. "Yep! Always known from birth that I am a lion. That's my Totem."

"I'm still confused. How long have you been able to do this? And where's the amulet?"

"I was only able to do it once things here changed. After I met Gar..."

"You mean after the forbidding fell?"

"Yes. When so much magic started flowing naturally, I could feel my Totem stirring, calling to me. Then the amulet just kind of focused that feeling and I was able to call the lion out."

"This amulet...can I see it?"

"Sure." He reached up to his neck, under his shirt, and removed a thin gold necklace with a tiny emerald stone attached. The filament of gold that made up the necklace strand was so fine that it almost disappeared against his mocha skin. He handed it to me and I held it up to the light in two hands.

I probed it gently with a thread of magic, listening for

its answering ping of mystical energy, trying to divine the source of the creation of such an amazing piece. It felt empty to me; no matter how I probed it, it gave off no signal, no residue of how it came to be. "Where did you get this?"

"I gave it to him." It was Esmay who spoke. She moved so silently that I didn't hear her as she entered the room. She was wiping her hands with a bloody towel as she locked her gaze on me. "It is protection against your probes, if that is what you are using right now."

"That would explain why he has always appeared as a normal human to me," I said. "I have never sensed anything of the supernatural about him, and I still don't."

Esmay nodded. "Exactly. The amulet is from a time and a magic that predates your own. It is a family heirloom, passed down for safekeeping. When Isla and I moved here, I felt it awaken, thanks to the rituals you had performed. You broke the spells that contained the original Shifter magic… and this amulet runs on a similar spell. When I knew it was awake, I gave it to Jhamal and began teaching him how to control his Totem."

"But what is he?" I asked again. "What exactly is a Totem?"

I saw Esmay look at Jhamal out of the corner of her eye and nod to the stairs. He rolled his eyes in response, but dutifully picked up his cup of coffee and bounded up the stairs. Esmay followed his step on the creaking floorboards until she heard him enter a room and close the door behind him.

"Jhamal is what is known as Otherkin," said Esmay. "Are you familiar with that term?"

I shook my head on my way to the Keurig as Esmay continued. "Otherkin are humans that self-identify as nonhuman. They believe themselves to be different, either genetically or as a result of reincarnation, trapped inside a human host. Some believe they are animals, either real or mythical, or creatures of the Fae world; fairy, elf, troll...you name it. The belief is so strong that they sometimes feel they can will their physical bodies to become the Totem within."

"And that's what Jhamal is...an Otherkin?"

Esmay took a breath before continuing. "You should know that in most cases, Otherkin is considered a psychiatric disorder. Many of them are seen as disassociated from normal society, suffering from a mental disorder that can be treated with certain drugs. Jhamal's parents treated him this way. They were concerned their son had suffered from some sort of mental break, and that he was under the delusion that he was an animal trapped in a human body. They considered him dangerous, and when he started to refuse his medication, they kicked him out of their home. They were also under the assumption that whatever mental issues created this affliction were the same ones that made him gay."

"Jesus," was all I could muster.

"Oh, that was part of their treatment plan as well—prayer and drugs to make everything okay."

I almost teared up, thinking about Gar and wondering how anyone could condemn another human being based on who they loved. "That's terrible. Who could treat their own child like that?"

"You'd be surprised," Esmay continued. "Jhamal and Isla have always been close, as you can imagine. He phoned her and asked if he could he stay with us. Of course we said yes, and that was the main reason we moved to this town. We showed up, picked him up at the youth center he was staying at, and decided to put down roots. Isla had also been informed that her aunt had died here, and she had inherited a large chunk of that estate."

I caught myself looking away from Esmay as she recounted this part of the story, and pretended to be focusing on cooling my coffee enough to drink. I blew listlessly at the dark, awful liquid swimming in the cup before I took a sip.

"So it wasn't just to take Dr. Garner Senior's place?" I asked.

"Oh no...that was a large part of it; it just wasn't all of it," said Esmay. "Isla is convinced there was foul play involved in her aunt's death, and so am I. We will find out what happened, believe me, but we also have a teenager to care for now as well."

"So are there more of them out there? More Totem Shifters?"

"That's a hard question to answer. There are many who self-identify as Otherkin, but they don't have amulets. But I've heard rumors…"

"Rumors? What kind of rumors?"

"Rumors that since the forbidden fell, there are some who have found different ways to transform into their true selves. But again, those are just rumors. One thing is for sure, however: more are going to be moving to Trinity Cove. When you broke the veil, you rang the dinner bell."

Esmay caught me looking wistfully at the back of the clinic. I blushed when I saw her staring.

"He'll be fine," she said. "Isla is really good at putting things back together again."

"Why hasn't she come to let me know how he's doing? Why is Kendra still back there but I can't be?"

"You saw how much blood he lost. Isla is probably using

Kendra as a donor. Shifter blood is pretty much universal when it comes to transfusions with other Shifters."

"Esmay…what happened to Cody back there? What did you see?"

She took a deep breath and moved to sit next to me. "Not much, to be honest with you. From the outside, it just looked like an abandoned building. Nothing stood out about it at all. But Kendra said she could smell blood and gunpowder inside. She said she could also feel Cody being tortured, and that he was in agonizing pain."

"Wait, what do you mean she could feel what was happening to him?" I interrupted.

Esmay shrugged. "I guess it's a Shifter thing. She could tell where he was in the building, and to a degree what he was feeling. We decided the best thing to do would be to send her to Cody, while Jhamal and I made as much noise as possible taking out the guards, in hopes it would draw away whoever was torturing Cody.

"A few concussion grenades plus a giant gold lion rampaging through the complex did the trick. That was when we stumbled across you. But I don't know exactly what was going on with Cody. You'll have to ask Kendra that."

I was about to respond when Kendra herself walked out of the back room and motioned for us. "Dr. Garner says you can come back to see him now."

"How is he?" I asked, barging into the treatment room. Cody was lying on the gurney, eyes closed. Both of his arms and chest were heavily bandaged. I was starting to hate this room. Too many times I had been here while someone close to me had lain there just like Cody.

"The damage looked worse than it actually was," said Isla. "I'm not sure what they used to cut him, but the blade was treated with some type of anticoagulant, or blood thinner, that I have never seen before. It was why he kept bleeding and couldn't heal."

"That means they knew he was a Shifter and were prepared to deal with him as such," said Esmay as she walked up to the bed. "Maybe this is something they have done to Shifters before. They know how to deal with supernaturals. Like silver bullets..." She trailed off, glancing at Kendra.

"The Warlock and Mallis said they were trying to get him back on their team...or some such bullshit," I said, reaching out to place a hand on Cody's.

"I'm sorry, what?" said Esmay. "You met Mallis?"

I looked around the room at all the eyes that were now focused on me. "Uh, yeah. I guess with all the commotion I forgot to mention that."

"And you're still alive," said Esmay. "Okay, that tells us a lot." She began pacing in the room, muttering softly to herself.

"What does it tell us?" I asked.

"That they either think they can't kill you, or there is still something they need from you," came Cody's weakened voice from the bed. He had opened his eyes and was looking around the room.

"Hey, don't try to move," said Kendra as she rushed to the other side of the bed. She placed a hand gently on his chest to let him know that he shouldn't even think about getting up. The intimacy of the gesture struck me oddly, and Kendra slowly withdrew her hand at the look on my face.

"Cody, they got the map...why were they torturing you?" I asked.

"They wanted me in their camp. This damn war they

keep going on about—it was either join them or die. They had some weird ceremonial-looking knife and they kept cutting me while some old lady was chanting. I don't know what they were doing, but it hurt like hell. I couldn't heal... the more they cut in into me the harder it became for me to stay conscious."

"Chanting? As in a spell?" Esmay asked, approaching Cody.

"Maybe," he replied. "Not really sure. I couldn't understand them."

"May I?" Esmay asked, pointing at Cody's bandages.

He nodded, and Esmay carefully removed one of the wrappings from his chest. I moved closer, trying to see what had her so enraptured. The bleeding had stopped and I could see the wounds already closing up.

"How did you stop the bleeding?" I asked.

"Once I realized what they had used on him, I treated Cody with simple, yet highly effective, oral-activated charcoal. It is used in the treatments of poison...it helps prevent them from being absorbed in the system. That is basically what the anticoagulants were doing: poisoning him. Once the charcoal was introduced, it allowed his body's healing abilities to kick into overdrive and stop the bleeding."

"What is it?" asked Cody, angling his head to see the part of his body that Esmay was examining.

"These cuts," Esmay said, "they aren't random."

I peered closer at Cody's torso and could see that she was right. Whoever had sliced him wasn't so much cutting into him as they were carving him. He was scoured in patterns; a thumbnail sliver of a moon, what appeared to be a half cross, marks that looked like the start of Egyptian hieroglyphs. "What the fuck?"

"Cipher magic," Esmay said, stepping back and

allowing Isla to redress Cody's wounds. "Ancient runes that are carved into living creatures and are combined with magical spells to bring that creature under the dominion of another. They are a path to locking away a being's free will."

"That's how the Warlock is controlling the Shifters," I said.

"Maybe," said Esmay. "At least the ones that aren't voluntarily following him. But it takes a lot of magic to power spells like this. Breaking free will is no easy task."

"I saw a witch there. Well, I felt one at least, held in one of the rooms of the warehouse. I couldn't get her free before we had to leave. That's why we have to go back!"

Esmay looked at me. She stopped herself from saying something.

"No," said Cody, his voice weak but leaving no room for arguing, "that's not happening…at least not right now."

"Cody, you don't understand. They are using that witch to power the Warlock's magic. She was nearly dead…I could feel it."

"And if you go back there right now, you'll be dead along with her. Or worse…you'll be his new battery. Imagine what he could do with you as a power source."

I didn't reply. What he said had the ring of truth to it. But still…I had promised her I would come back.

Cody leaned forward, no doubt sensing my thoughts. "Allie, we can't do this again without a better plan. That she-wolf took out both of us without so much as breaking a sweat. We need a better plan before we go in there."

"He's right," said Esmay. "I know what it means to you to help whoever was in there, and I promise that I'll help you in any way I can, but right now is not the time. They will have called back their reinforcements and the whole building will be on lockdown. Also, more likely than not, they will move tonight. That base is compromised and there is no way a vampire will stay in a den that has been breached by a witch.

"By the time we get back there, the sun will be setting, and I guarantee he will be gone the second that happens."

I took a breath to steady my beating heart. They were both right, of course. Deep down I knew that. Just like I also knew that most likely that witch only had hours left to live, judging by how faint her life-force was. But that didn't make it right.

"There is still one thing we need to do," I said. "We have to warn all of the families whose homes I shielded. They aren't safe."

"Leave that to me," said Kendra. "I'll take some of the Shifters at the camp that I can trust, and we'll head out to the sites. If there are Shifters living there, they should have our backs and believe us. If there are witches...well, hopefully the same scenario will play out. We can round them up, head into the hills. Weather's still warm at night up by the Falls. We will head there. Safety in numbers."

I nodded and thanked her. "I'll go with you. This is my fault, after all. It's the least I can do to help make it right."

"Don't think like that," said Cody. "And if you're going, so am I."

He moved to get out of the bed, grimacing and clutching at his ribcage.

"That would be a negative, mister," said Dr. Garner. "You are staying here overnight. I need to make sure all of that blood thinner is out of your system before you go taxing yourself."

"Rest," I said gently to him. "I promise I will not go off half-cocked by myself. I just need to do this." He nodded and lay back against the pillow. "Esmay, can we borrow your car? I need to swing by my house so I can check on Gar."

"I can have Jhamal bring him here for tonight," said Esmay. "He'll be safe and under two watchful eyes."

After considering for a moment, I nodded in agreement. I knew Cody would protect Gar with his life, and after seeing what a Totem Shifter was capable of, I felt even more at ease knowing he would be under the same roof as one.

"Well then," I said to Kendra. "Looks like it's you and me. Let's go up to the encampment and see if we can start building a little army of our own."

Chapter Seventeen

"You know, I'm not after your man." Kendra took her eyes off the road long enough to look over at me.

I felt sheepish; a warm fire was creeping across my cheeks. "I'm sorry. I had no right to imply that."

"Are you kidding? You had every right. Believe me, I've been on the receiving end of that before…I would never do it to someone else. Ever."

It was the thousand-pound Elephant-Shifter sitting in the car with us, and I was glad it had finally been acknowledged. "You've been a good friend to me, Kendra. I don't know why I let my head go there. It's just that I have never been in a relationship before. I mean, not a real one. Schoolgirl crushes did not prepare me for this."

She laughed, and again glanced over at me. "I'm sorry that you are going through all of this, Allie."

I smiled. She had no idea how much those simple words meant to me. "Thank you, Kendra. I'm sorry that you've been dragged into this."

She shrugged, adjusting both hands on the steering

wheel. "It's okay. Honestly, when I moved here, it was to forget my past. To start over. Once I found myself being able to Shift, I knew I had to get away from a bad situation. I mean, it's one thing to fantasize about being able to one day fight back. But it's another matter entirely when you realize that you could accidentally decapitate your abusive husband with a single swipe of your paw if you got carried away. Plus, being a Shifter gave me the strength to walk away and know that I would be fine out there."

"What made you come here to Trinity Falls?"

"Not sure. I was drawn to the eastern part of the States. Plus, there were all kinds of rumors going around the internet about a tiny town in North Carolina that had brought magic back for a lot of supernaturals. I wasn't the only one that heard those rumors. But the time I got here, the encampment was already forming up near the Falls. Shifters from all over the country were moving here."

"Why stay up there? All of you would be more than welcome in town."

"Those among us that are old enough to remember the days before the Warlocks are hesitant to trust the humans again. Those of us who had never known this life of a Shifter are too unsure to challenge their wisdom."

That was understandable. As much as I loved magic, I would never dream of second-guessing my aunts. They had a lifetime of knowledge and practice on me.

"So…" said Kendra, "what exactly is a Reliquary?"

"Where did you hear that?" I asked.

"At the warehouse. Two of the creeps that were torturing Cody were saying something about his girlfriend being one and how that changed the stakes of the game… or something like that."

"All witches are born with the innate power to work with

and manipulate certain laws of magic, depending on what sign they are born into—Earth, Fire, Air, Water—and each sign determines what their power leans toward. Some have an affinity for Earth-based magic with herbs and potions. Some are able to use the more aggressive, Fire-based spells, some Air, some Water. A Reliquary is a witch that is born into all signs. I am not bound by spells and enchantments. I can call on the raw force of the magic all around me, and shape it as I desire. A Reliquary can contain and draw on nearly infinite amounts of magic...at least that's what I've been told." I looked out the window as the dust embers of dusk danced across the flashing landscape. "But I don't feel very powerful. I can't seem to save anyone. I can't stop a Warlock and a vampire...and I couldn't save a captive witch..." I swallowed the lump in my throat and fought back tears.

"Oh, I don't know about all that. You seem pretty damn powerful to me. I doubt I'd be here if it weren't for you, so I'm thankful. Can I ask...was your mother a Reliquary as well?"

I nodded. "I believe so. She was powerful enough to erect that forbidding and keep the Warlock imprisoned all these years."

"And she was better at this than you?" I stirred uncomfortably and she immediately clarified her statement. "No, I didn't mean that like that. I mean, she had to learn, right? She and your aunts practiced magic for a very long time before they had to draw upon it in battle. But you...you've had no one to teach you, from what I heard. You are running on pure instinct...and if that's the case, you cannot be hard on yourself. That's a hell of a learning curve to make up."

"I have never thought about it like that. But still...my

fear is that I don't have time to learn. A lunatic vampire with a Warlock and an army of Shifters has declared war on us and all of humanity. I need the Cliff Notes version of this magic shit."

"We're here," Esmay said unexpectedly. Nothing like a crippling case of self-doubt to make time fly.

Esmay eased the SUV off the main road and onto a dirt path that would take us to the camping area where the Shifters were staying. She rolled the vehicle to a stop and she turned to look at me one last time. "If they say no…"

"I'm not going to push it. God knows I understand where they would be coming from."

We trekked from the car to the edge of the encampment. I reached out with my magic…everything felt as it should. I could sense Kendra doing the same with her senses. Satisfied, we entered the camp, to be greeted warmly by those that were gathered outside of their homes, enjoying the silence that descends upon the woods at dusk.

"Kendra! You're okay!" said the old woman that I had met the night of the fires. "We were so worried!"

"I'm fine, Celest," Kendra said, leaning in to hug the smaller woman, "thanks to Allie and her friends."

"Thank you," said the woman. She motioned for the young boy that was hiding at the back of the crowd to come forward as well. It was the child that had been carried away by one of the wolves. "This is Jackson. He is all that remains of my family. I owe you a debt that I will never be able to repay." Her eyes grew moist, and I found my heart swelling in sympathy for the old woman.

"Why are we thanking her?" came a gruff voice from the assemblage. "She put us on the Warlock's radar. If it wasn't for her, we would not be hunted as we are now."

"If it weren't for her, you wouldn't be able to Shift now.

Her magic brought down the barrier between us and the power that needed to be whole again." It was Kendra. She stepped forward, her hands at her side and clenched into fists.

"We didn't ask to be cast back into this world," said the same deep voice. This time a man stepped forward. He was tall and had the girth of an oak barrel. But I knew it wasn't fat...I had a feeling that he was all solid muscle as he lumbered up to us. "I am Jasper Keen and I am a Bear-Shifter. I came here from Nebraska because I woke up in the middle of the woods one night with a fresh deer carcass split open in front of me. My hands were still covered in steaming intestines; I didn't know what was happening to me. Then I felt a calling...a need to head east. I followed my instincts and ended up here. But I don't know this world. I don't want to be a part of it."

"Jasper," said the old woman, "this young lady has made you whole. Show some gratitude."

"Young lady?" he replied. "You mean young witch? That's what she is, right? A witch—one that has played around with magic that I'm betting she does not understand."

A murmur of agreement moved through the crowd of Shifters. I was getting more than a little nervous, and one look at Kendra told me she was as well.

"Then go back, Jasper," Kendra shouted, her voice cutting a swath of silence through the crowd. "Why don't you leave? Is it because you have nowhere else to go? Or is it because deep down you feel a sense of community here?" She turned her back on the big man and addressed the assemblage. "The truth is, this was going to happen no matter what. Sooner or later, the forbidding that held back our true selves would have fallen. And then what? We would have found ourselves being hunted anyway. Here, we have one another. There is safety in numbers and we have the chance to dictate our future. I wasn't around during the time of the battle between the Warlocks and the witches. I don't remember any good old days. But I remember being afraid every day for my life, feeling weak and hopeless...yet in the back of my mind thinking that there was something more out there that I was meant to be part of. I didn't know I was a Shifter, but I knew I was more...and I am willing to bet that most of you felt that as well." A wave of agreement began to sweep through the Shifters before she continued. "I would rather die than go back to my old life. But if you want that—" she swung around to face Jasper again "—then go back to it. Go back to your dead life and stay there. But for me, this is where I choose to be myself...and I will fight to help make a better life for those who will come along after us. They—" she pointed at the young boy who now clung to the old woman's robes "—deserve better than we were allowed to have."

I couldn't have been more proud of my friend, and I moved to stand beside her. "Kendra is right. The Warlock has once again found his way into this world, and he, along with his dark master, the vampire known as Mallis, intends to make slaves of you—or kill you. I am not one of you, and yes, I was the one who ultimately freed the Warlock. But I did it to save someone that I love, someone that is one of you. And I would do the same thing again for any of you. I just can't fight this coming madness alone.

"I can't make you fight; I can only ask for your help. And in return I pledge every ounce of power in my possession to ridding this world of the Warlock and his ilk once and for all...making each and every one of you free—free to be who and what you really are...free to live openly among the humans. Together, we can create our own destiny...out loud and in the open, not hiding here in the woods.

"Kendra said there is safety in numbers...well, there is also strength in numbers. That's why I am here tonight. I need that strength. Together, we can stop the blackness that the Warlock and Mallis are threatening. But we have to work together."

Silence greeted me; I made up my mind that, despite what I had promised Cody, I would be heading back into that hellish warehouse alone. But then, the old woman cleared her throat and spoke up.

"I am a Fox-Shifter. I may no longer have the eyesight I did in my youth. My reflexes are a shadow of what they once were. My fangs are mostly for show at this point. But what breath I have left in these old lungs I will spend fighting at your side, young Allie." With that, she shifted into the form of a greying old fox, large of build but slight of muscle. She stood defiantly next to the young boy, her tired eyes sparkling defiantly in the early night.

Slowly, a few of the other members in the crowd stepped forward and nodded at me before shifting into their animal forms as well. A large badger appeared alongside two mountain lions. A German shepherd and two more Fox-Shifters also appeared; all of them stepped forward in greeting. Members of the crowd parted as another giant of a man stepped forward. Jasper placed a hand on his arm as if to hold him back. The man smiled gently at Jasper before taking his hand off his arm and stepping forward. He nodded to me, and shifted into a massive grizzly. A Tiger-Shifter and a majestic eagle appeared next to him.

I blinked away tears as I nodded back at my newfound allies. I watched in sadness as Jasper turned his back, and pushed his way to the back of the gathering where he disappeared into the darkness. Biting my tongue, I noticed a few others joined him, heading off into the approaching night. This would have to do...I could only pray we would be enough.

Just then, I felt a buzzing in my pocket and took my phone out. Cody's name and cell number flashed on the screen.

"What's up, Cody?"

"Allie. I just received a dispatch call...you need to meet me over to Hope's house. Now."

Chapter Eighteen

My heart was trip-hammering as Kendra sped us back into town. We didn't speak a word to one another during the drive. Honestly, I don't think I even breathed. Cody wouldn't tell me what was going on—he just said that he would meet me there.

But I could tell from his tone that whatever was going on, it wasn't good.

This was confirmed when we pulled through the gates of Hope's community, and were immediately greeted with throngs of neighbors, flashing lights, and various media vans setting up remote uplinks along the street. Kendra pulled as close as possible to Hope's house, and I was horrified to see the number of police cars, ambulances and firetrucks blocking the road. I didn't even let the car come to a complete stop before I was out and running down the street.

I pushed my way through neighbors crowding the sidewalks and ran toward the front door of Hope's house. At the last minute I felt a strong hand reach out and grab my elbow. I spun around and came face to face with Cody.

"Cody! What the hell? What happened here?" My voice was frantic and I searched Cody's features for any clue as to what was happening.

"Allie…I need you to be strong now."

Fuck. "Cody. Is it Hope…is she…"

He took a deep breath and placed both hands on my arms, willing me to look him in the eyes. "Hope is not hurt. It's…it's her parents, Allie. It's not good."

I shook Cody off and ran for the door. The policeman standing guard outside of it raised a hand, but he must have seen signal from Cody over my shoulder because he then just stepped aside to let me enter.

The first thing I noticed was the amount of yellow tape that was stretched throughout Hope's house. Then I noticed the number of people inside, some taking pictures of everything, some scribbling in notepads, and others talking rapidly on their phones. I looked through the great room to the double French doors that led to the patio and pool area. The great room was covered in glass and wood from the doors. Splotches of red dotted the hardwood, leading in a line toward the back hall—the hall that led to the master suite.

"…caught the female here and then she ran to the bedroom…" one of the men inside the house was saying to someone. I saw him pointing at the line of blood.

I steeled myself, tried to command my heart to slow down. How fast could the human heart beat? I felt like mine was about to leap out of my chest at any moment as I walked down the hall toward the bedroom. There were voices coming from inside, but I couldn't make them out over the sound of my own blood rushing to my head.

I stepped into the space and gasped, throwing a hand over my mouth to stifle a scream and choking back the bile that threatened to erupt from me. My body began to tremble all over as I took in the grisly scene. The once beautiful master retreat, with its soft linens, contemporary furniture, and graceful palladium windows had been desecrated. Blood and bits of human flesh were everywhere. The wall, the windows, the area rugs...even the vaulted ceiling had not been spared.

My eyes were immediately drawn to the king-sized bed with the large, gray linen headboard. Hope's mother—or what was left of her—was splayed open on the bed. Her torso had been ripped apart, and one leg was missing. What remained of her beautiful face was turned to one side, her mouth agape in a soundless, horrifying scream.

The flash of a camera and more voices were coming from the en suite bath. I could make out something along the lines of "...I think this was the husband..." but I could not bring myself to go in there. I backed out of the room slowly, and ran right into Cody, who had come up behind me. Spinning around, I buried my face in his chest, welcoming his strong arms as they embraced me.

"What...what happened? And where is Hope?"

"We aren't sure what happened exactly...Hope is out back with a detective and a couple of paramedics."

"Paramedics? Was she hurt too?"

"No. She's in shock, Allie. She hasn't said a word."

I broke away from him and ran back to the great room. I made my way slowly through the broken glass, ignoring the annoyed looks I received from the detective. I assumed Cody must have let everyone know who I was, because none of them stopped me from tramping through their crime scene. Either that or they knew, just like I was beginning to suspect, that whatever did this would not be caught via normal police procedure.

I found Hope sitting on one of the patio chairs on the far side of the pool. There was a paramedic with a clipboard seated next to her, and another lady with long hair pulled back in a ponytail and a small spiral notebook in one hand. I assumed she was the detective Cody had told me about.

I moved close to Hope before the detective could stop me, and squatted down in front of her so that my face was inches from her own. Her eyes were open, but staring far off into the distance. Her face was emotionless, yet vulnerable. I reached out and placed my hands on her arms, giving them a gentle squeeze. Tears flooded my face as I tried to reach my best friend.

"Hope. Hey, girl...it's me, Allie. Can you hear me?" Her glassy eyes remained fixed in the distance. There was no rigidity in her frame as I rubbed her arms in desperation. "What's wrong with her?" I said to the two women next to us.

"She's in a state of shock," said the detective. "She came home...and found them."

"Oh my God," I replied, returning my gaze to Hope. "Hope...I am so sorry this happened to you. Can you hear me?"

She didn't reply, but I saw something; a spark in her eyes, a trace of acknowledgement. Slowly her eyes began to focus, and locked on me. Something sparked; maybe it was recognition, or maybe it was a memory of something so painful it had caused her to instantly seal off the world. Too late, I realized, it was neither.

It was anger.

The sudden sting of her hand as it swept across my face

shocked me to my core. Then she was screaming. Still inches from my face, she yelled at the top of her lungs, and drew back her hand to strike me again. I fell back on my backside as I tried to protect my face from the blows she rained down on me...all the while cursing and yelling like a madwoman.

The detective and the paramedic grabbed her, and between them were able to pull her back into the chair.

"Hold her still!" said the paramedic. "I'm going to give her a sedative!" She reached into the tackle box that sat alongside the chair, and hurriedly found a syringe, which she used to draw up a clear fluid from a vial.

"Noooooo!" Hope wailed, her voice raw and pained, seeming to have been ripped from the depths of her soul. "How could you do this? You were my friend!"

I sat there shocked, completely aware of how comical I might have looked in a different situation: my hair was disheveled, and I held one hand against my burning cheek, mouth agape.

By now, another detective had appeared and was helping to restrain Hope as the paramedic worked on getting the injection into her arm.

"You did this!" Hope screamed at me. "You brought your monsters into my life and now they've butchered my family! This is all your fault, witch! I told you...I told you..." She trailed off as the sedative started to take effect. A second paramedic appeared with a stretcher, and they slowly eased Hope onto it. Once she was lying flat, they strapped her down and covered her with a blanket. "I trusted you," she cried, closing her eyes as her head lolled to one side.

I stood and watched as they rolled my friend away.

"We have to get her to the hospital," said one of the

paramedics to the detective as they rushed her away and back through the house.

I could only watch, numb from the shock. I felt Cody's arm engulf me, but in all honesty he might as well have not even been there.

The roar of my own blood swirling around inside my head was all I could make out. Voices were slow to penetrate my internal din, and from what seemed like a great distance I heard voices directed at me.

"I'm sorry, what?" I said, looking around to see who was speaking. It was Detective Ponytail.

"I said I need to speak with you." She flipped open her book and began scribbling. "She called you Allie, correct? As in Allison Caine?" I nodded and she scribbled again.

"Um, Detective..." began Cody, before being cut off by a single look from Ponytail.

"Allie, what just happened here? Why did your friend just say that you were responsible for the murder of her parents?"

I felt my eyes well up again as I turned to face her. "I don't know. You said it yourself, she was in shock."

"The operative word in that statement is was," she replied. "She certainly seemed to snap out of it when you came around."

"I...I don't know what happened here," I managed.

"No, maybe you don't know exactly what happened, but I'm willing to bet you know something."

"Detective, this has been a shock for everyone involved," said Cody. "Her best friend's parents were just brutally murdered. This can wait until tomorrow."

"Can it, Officer Cody?" she replied. "If you say so. But I'm betting the sooner we get some kind of statement from your friend, the better."

"I already told you," I hissed, "I don't know anything about this."

The detective nodded and closed her notebook. "All right. Well, how about you tell me something you do know about. Like werewolves."

Chapter Nineteen

You would think after the trauma we had just been through, the least they would have done at the police station would have been to turn the heat up a little. The A/C was blasting, and despite my jacket, I was beginning to shiver. I started to wonder if it was part of police procedure to make the interrogation room as cold as possible. Or was it to turn up the heat to make the suspect sweat it out? Who the fuck knew.

As many times as I had stopped by the department to drop off muffins for Cody or just to say hi, I had never realized how big the station was. For such a tiny town, it was shocking. I never knew there was a basement, and certainly would have never guessed that it was where all the holding cells and interrogation rooms were. I sat in one by myself, freezing, waiting for Detective Ponytail—or someone—to come and shine a bright light in my eyes, threaten me with never seeing daylight again…etc. At least not until I gave them all the information I had.

Before my overactive imagination could finish running

through every episode of CSI to play out what would happen next, the door to the small room opened. As I had expected, Detective Ponytail walked in. But as I had not expected, she brought with her a cup of steaming hot coffee and a couple of scones on a tray. I eyed them suspiciously, but she only smiled and nodded at me.

"Don't worry, Allie; we aren't going to drug you," she said as she pulled out a chair on the other side of the tiny table where I sat. "Jesus, it's cold down here…" She took out her cell phone and keyed in a number. "Hey, Jim, what's up with the A/C down here? It's like a meat locker. Okay, we'd appreciate it." She hung up and almost instantly I heard the whoosh of blowing air stop and felt it replaced with a stream of warmth.

"Thank you," I murmured.

The detective nodded at the tray. "I'm afraid they aren't as good as the ones you serve, but I figured you might be hungry." She made it clear that nothing more was going to happen until I at least had something to eat. I obliged by taking a bite out of a scone—it was orange-marmalade-flavored—and then a sip of the coffee. The scone was god-awful and nearly choked me, but at least the coffee made up for it.

The detective smiled and leaned forward, placing a notebook on the table before her. "My name is Dana Walters, and I'm a homicide detective, Ms. Caine. I'm sorry we had to meet under such undesirable circumstances."

Despite my suspicion, she sounded sincere. I put the coffee cup down and looked directly into her amber eyes. "Detective Walters, I swear to you I had nothing to do with this."

"I know." The finality of her statement shook me. "We

spoke with Officer Hunter, and honestly, even without his statement we knew you had nothing to do with this."

"Then why am being detained here?" I asked.

"Because I need your help," she said, placing both elbows on the table and leaning forward. "I need answers and I have nowhere else to turn."

"Answers? To what?"

"To what the hell is happening to this town lately, for starters. Why does such a picturesque, sleepy town need the services of a Queen City homicide detective and her full team? Why have the incidents of unexplained acts of arson, theft, kidnapping and murder grown so high in Trinity Cove —in a matter of months?"

I didn't say anything, just kept my eyes cast downward at the scones in front of me. Her words made my throat drier than if I had tried to shove all of them in my mouth at once.

Detective Walters sat back in her chair and regarded me silently for a moment. "Okay, I get it. You must have your reasons for not wanting to talk to me. But let me just say that, believe it or not, we are on the same side here. I just want all the bad shit that's going down around here to stop."

I looked around, still trying to decide how much I should trust her. "That's what I want as well. But...it's not that easy."

"It never is, for one person acting alone. Tell me how I can help. What happened to your friend's parents tonight?"

The mention of Hope made me tense up all over again. I refused, however, to let this stranger see me cry. "Can you at least tell me if Hope is all right first?"

"She was admitted for observation. But she should be

fine. At least...as fine as anyone can be, considering what she has been through."

"What happened? I mean, did she call 911 or was it someone else?"

Detective Walters flipped open her notebook and scanned a few pages before answering. "From what we have been able to put together, someone broke into her parents' house at approximately 7:45. That is when the home alarm system registered broken glass; but the alarm was not set, so there was no automatic call to the security house."

"No. Her parents were bad about not arming the alarm system until they went to bed for the night."

She nodded before continuing. "The perpetrator, or perpetrators, broke in through the back French doors. There were signs of a struggle with the female in the great room. Her mother must have fought back before fleeing into the bedroom. That was where her husband was. He was in the shower at the time and may not have heard the initial scuffle in the great room. The perp followed her into the bedroom and there..." I waved her off. I had seen all the gory details...I didn't need to hear them. "The husband was cornered in the bath by the same perp or perps, and... well, let's just say that what was done to his wife paled in comparison to what they did to him."

I swallowed hard, mentally shutting down my third eye. "Detective, who could have done that?" I needed to know just how much she knew.

She regarded my wryly, as if to say, Okay, I see your hundred and raise you a grand. "C'mon, Allie. I thought we were beyond this. We both know this atrocity was not committed by a who, but a what. That woman's limb was ripped off her body. Not cut off; torn off. I don't know about you, but I don't know any human being capable of doing that, even ones that are high on heroin...and, for the record, that's the working theory about this attack right now."

"What? That they were killed in a robbery by some desperate drug addicts? Jesus. If it's not a random, stray animal attack, then it's drug addicts high on God knows what kind of shit."

"There has been a lot of that in this town lately. I don't buy it. Tell me what's really going on."

I hesitated for a second, but then was overcome with a wave of weariness. Fuck it. Let's see just how open her mind really is.

"All right then," I said. "I think my best friend's parents were killed by werewolves. Or maybe vampires. But you already suspected that, didn't you?"

She exhaled and leaned back, locking her eyes to mine. "Vampires? For real? I guess that shouldn't come as a surprise. If werewolves are real...then why not?"

"There is a war brewing, and Trinity Cove is ground zero."

"War? What kind of war?"

"There's an age-old vampire named Mallis. He has a Warlock apprentice helping him gather an army of Shifters. Mallis plans to black out the sun so he is not longer contained to roaming only at night. He will use his Warlock to gather enough witches so that he can harness their power and cast a darkening spell. Then, with no sunlight to stop him, he and his followers will spread out, destroying and assimilating any and all life on earth. Or some such shit."

Detective Walters was quiet for a moment as she contemplated.

"Crazy, huh?" I said.

"I've heard crazier. You don't sound like you believe it is going to happen."

"A spell to blot out the sun? No, I don't think it is possible. But...I do think a lot more innocents are going to die before this is over." In my mind I could see that horrific scene in Hope's house. I could once again smell the suffocating scent of blood and entrails filling my nose. I shuffled uncomfortably in my seat, ready for this interrogation to be over.

"So where do you fit into all of this? I assume there must be a connection; otherwise, why would they come after your best friend's parents?"

"I don't think they were after them. I think they were after Hope—to send me a message."

"What message?"

"To stay out of this. I...trespassed on their territory today and did some damage. I think they wanted payback."

"So...you're a witch? The rumors are true?"

I nodded, suddenly unable to trust my voice.

"You plan to fight this vampire? Alone?"

I shifted my weight from one butt cheek to the other. This time I didn't answer.

"What did your friend mean when she said you 'brought these monsters to her'?"

"That's a longer story that I'm not sure I can tell you just yet. But I didn't do any of this on purpose."

She nodded. I could tell that she wanted to press me on the matter, but something told her to let it go—at least for now.

"Fair enough. Look, I already have Officer Cody Hunter's statement. I know that whatever strange goings-on are happening in this town, he seems to be running point... or at least running interference, for you. Some of the other officers are saying that the unofficial rule is that the two of you take lead on the more…'out there' cases. True?"

I nodded silently.

"Then he must trust you. And I trust him. But I have to ask; do you have support?"

"I do now. I have a couple of friends that are helping me. Plus, there is a community of Shifters that have moved into the area. I have reached out to them for help."

"Shifters? Like werewolves?"

"No wolves. But a few others that will be valuable." I didn't want to press that. No need to give up the Shifter location, especially since they were out rounding up the supernaturals I had put in harm's way.

The door opened, and Cody came in. He looked exhausted and worried. No doubt he still wasn't completely healed, and for a moment I felt guilty about that as well.

"Detective…are we good? You have your answers." He had obviously been listening in somewhere.

"I have some answers," she replied. "I have a feeling that Allie here as just provided me with more questions—but we can save those for another time."

"Why aren't you more freaked out?" I asked. "Why are you accepting all of this so readily?"

She sighed and pushed her seat back away from the table. "Because I grew up in this town. My father ran with an unsavory bunch. And he used to tell me all kinds of stories about the residents of Trinity Cove from back in the day."

She stood up, closed her notebook, and walked toward the door. She paused as she placed one hand on the doorknob and turned to give me one last glance.

"Plus, he was a werewolf as well."

Chapter Twenty

I was exhausted by the time we headed back to my house. I insisted that Cody stop at Dr. Garner's so that I could pick up Gar.

"He's perfectly safe where he is," Cody said.

"I don't care. He's not as safe as he would be with me." I was feeling stubborn and more than a little on edge.

"He's with a Lion-Shifter and, in case you didn't notice, Esmay is pretty damn good with that sword of hers."

I tried not to let my annoyance show, but it slipped through. "Rapier. It's not a sword."

"Sorry. Rapier."

I looked away, trying to contain myself. "Can you please just stop so we can take him back to the house with us?"

He swung the car around in silence, and for once, I was grateful for the quiet.

Esmay greeted us at the door. She knew that I had been taken in for questioning, and had a few questions of her own.

"I'm fine," I reassured her, "just exhausted. I made Cody stop here to get Gar. Is he okay?"

"He's fine," she replied. "He doesn't know what happened. But I think he could tell from the mood that something is off. He'll probably hit you up later for some details."

Yes. He would. I struggled, but knew that the right thing to do would be to tell him the truth.

He was still half-asleep as he groggily walked out the door, thanking Esmay and Isla for their hospitality. Before joining him, I addressed Esmay one last time.

"Oh yeah, see what you can find out about a Detective Dana Walters; she works out of Queen City and is investigating all the goings-on here in Trinity. Her father was part of the Shifter community." Esmay arched a single, exquisitely manicured eyebrow, but then just nodded. I gave her a quick hug and then followed Gar out to the car.

Cody was silent behind the wheel as he fired up the engine and we headed toward home. Gar was in the backseat, his head slumped to the side in a weird, uncomfortable-looking position. Boys can fall asleep anywhere. Or so I thought.

"So," he grumbled without opening his eyes, "what's wrong? And don't feed me a line about everything being cool, because it obviously ain't."

I could feel Cody look over at me as he opened his mouth to say something. I placed one hand on his thigh and gave it a gentle pat, letting him know this was for me to answer.

"I got careless, Gar. This vampire Mallis and the Warlock are waging a very serious, very deadly game with us. And I played right into their hands." I told him everything that had happened, from my ill-conceived plan to cast a protection spell over the undisclosed supernaturals in the area, and ending with my interrogation in the holding room at police headquarters about the horrific events at Hope's house.

"My God," he said, obviously shaken. "Poor Hope! Her mother…she was always so kind to me…she…" He trailed off, tears slipping down his face. "Holy shit, I'm glad you were there for her. She's in shock after what just happened. She'll come around. You're her best friend, after all."

"I'm the best friend that got her parents murdered," I said quietly.

He scooched forward on his seat enough to throw his arms around my shoulders from behind. "You are the best friend and the best big sister anyone could ever ask for. You're a boss in my book!"

I turned in my seat to get a better look at him. "What?"

"I said my sister is the boss. Those were baller moves you made! Fucking going up against a major vamp like that. Taking out his hideout. Brass moves, sis."

None of that was what I would have called brass moves, and I turned back around in my seat. Out of the corner of my eye I could see Cody smirking.

I was happy I had told Gar everything. Well, almost everything. I had left out the part about Jhamal being the Lion-Shifter that had saved me. That was a bridge I didn't think was my right to cross. But I also didn't want to tiptoe around it.

"So," I began, "you and Jhamal do anything fun? Did you see him or was he helping out at the vet clinic?"

"No, he didn't work today," said Gar.

I nodded, not sure how far to probe. "You know, I'm sorry we picked you up early. It's just that after what happened at Hope's, I needed to make sure you were safe."

"I was safe with Jhamal. A Lion Totem-Shifter is nothing to screw around with," he said matter-of-factly.

"Wait...you know about him?" I asked.

"Of course. He told me everything as soon as we started to get serious."

"And you didn't think to tell me?"

"Why should I? That's not my secret to tell." He sat back and closed his eyes. "Allie? Can I go see Hope tomorrow? I really feel like she probably needs all the hugs she can get right now."

I felt too guilty to do anything other than just nod.

We pulled up to the house...and as soon as I stepped out of the car, I felt it.

"What is it?" said Cody, sensing the sudden tension in my body.

"My wards," I said. "They're down. Gar, stay in the car." For once, he didn't question me as he dove back into the seat. I heard the click of the door locks being thrown.

I gathered a brace of magic and kept it flowing into my hand, ready to be unleashed at a moment's notice. Cody had shifted to his hybrid form, claws extended and at the ready.

We made our way up the porch and I reached for the door slowly, glancing over at Cody. He nodded, reassuring me that whatever was inside, we would face together. Just as I was about to touch the handle, the heavy door swung open.

Aunt Vivian stood inside, a large welcoming grin on her face.

"Now I know I taught you the proper way to say hello, Allie, and that is most definitely not it," she said.

I couldn't do anything but drop my magic as I flew into her outstretched arms, my tears flowing freely.

Chapter Twenty-One

After my admittedly shame-free sob-fest, Aunt Lena and Aunt Vivian put Gar to bed amidst quite a bit of whispering and giggling. Then, they returned back to the spacious kitchen where Aunt Lena went about setting a kettle for tea. Cody and I sat at the large island and watched the two sisters work in unison to prepare drinks and a plate of cut fruits for us.

"So," began Aunt Vivian, "what have you done, Allie?"

I wasn't sure where to begin, and the look on my face must have been more than a little troubling to her, because she walked around the island and threw a protective arm around my shoulders.

"We felt it," she continued, "the raw power you were messing with. We tried to get back sooner, but we were busy with the counsel up in New England; we were trying to convince them that the Warlocks were back, and all witches were once again in danger. They won't take action, however. They see this as the actions of a single supernatural, possibly a Warlock that seems to have a blood vendetta against our family."

"If you ask me, I say they are just chicken shit. If this Warlock were running amuck in their fancy little Connecticut towns or lovely New York hamlets, they would organize and take his ass out," quipped Aunt Lena as she set two cups of tea in front of me and Cody.

"Sister! Language," replied Aunt Vivian. "But yes...the actions of a lone Warlock do not concern the council at this time."

"But how can that be?" I asked. "Surely they realize that if one Warlock has returned, there will be more to follow. And more Warlocks mean more witches that will be enslaved and ultimately killed."

"They have their reasons for staying out of this," said Aunt Vivian.

"Yes, it very political," added Aunt Lena. "They have been at odds with our family for generations. We don't exactly see eye to eye. Your mother was in line to be the next Grand Leader of the Council. Her birthright as a Reliquary demanded that. But when she broke rank, refused to have anything to do with the council, refused to let them have anything to do with you...well, that didn't sit too well with them."

"That was why they refused to help during the last attack on Trinity," said Aunt Vivian. "That was why we were on our own. They see the sacrifice your mother made as one that was her decision and responsibility to make. They pretty much cut Trinity off after that."

"And that is why we will probably be on our own again," said Aunt Lena. I could hear the exhaustion in her voice, and part of me felt guilty for allowing them to comfort me when it should have been the other way around.

For the second time that night, I found myself vomiting up the details of my recent actions. My aunts listened intently, never once interrupting my narrative with questions. When I finished, I sat back and waited for the inevitable tongue-lashing.

"Interesting," said Aunt Lena.

"Very," added Aunt Vivian. "Using locator magic like that was ingenious. And adding a protective barrier around the homes was inspiring. Although, in truth, it was probably not needed."

"Why not?" I said. "They needed to be protected."

"Shifters, even the ones that are new to their abilities, have a preternatural sense for danger. They sense magic, especially malicious magic. I'm betting as soon as you cast your spell, it freaked them out so much that many left their homes right away." Aunt Vivian took a long sip of her tea before continuing. "I am so very sorry to hear about Hope's parents. They were good people. No one deserves to die that way."

"How is that poor girl doing?" asked Aunt Lena.

It seemed too indifferent for me to shrug, so I just didn't say anything. That didn't seem enough for them, so finally I murmured something about Hope asking me to keep my distance, in so many words.

"Allie," said Aunt Lena, letting a little admonishment creep into her voice for the first time, "that girl, your best friend, just went through an unimaginable trauma. She is alone right now. I don't want to think what she must be feeling. She needs to be surrounded by those who love and know her best—and that's not the counselors and nurses at the hospital."

"But it was my fault! I mean...she was right; I brought the Warlock here. I freed the Shifters. I picked a fight with

Mallis...what happened to her was a message meant for me."

"I don't think it was," said Aunt Vivian.

"What do you mean?" I asked.

"That Warlock and Mallis had you in their hands. Both of you," she added, addressing Cody. "But they didn't kill you. That means they either have plans for you...or they weren't sure how to kill you."

"My bet would be the former," said Aunt Lena. "A Warlock drains and uses a witch. Then he kills her once she serves no purpose. And you are a Reliquary witch. He would have had special plans for someone like you. I think Mallis wanted to figure out a way to use you. A Leveling is a very powerful magical working; for a Warlock to even consider pulling it off, it would require him to tap into an equally powerful mystical source."

"Someone like Allie," said Cody, speaking up for the first time.

"Wait, so are you saying that what that crazy vamp is planning is actually possible?" I said.

Aunt Vivian shrugged her shoulders. "Who knows. Technically, it could be possible given the right spells, right magic source, and right timing."

"Timing?" asked Cody. "What do you mean?"

"Well," said Aunt Lena, "if he wants to blot out the sun, he will need some help from cosmic alignment. A Leveling is the magical equivalent of an extinction-level event. Everything has to align in the cosmos to make it happen. The Warlock can't just gather some power and command the sun to stop shining."

"So what is the confluence of events that would make it possible?" I asked.

"I have no idea. It would have to be something natural,

and from there, the leveling would take hold, and corrupt nature...creating a new set of laws to be followed."

Cody jumped to his feet and grabbed at his phone, swiping and tapping on it like crazy. He looked up at us, eyes wide. "Something like an eclipse?"

We all looked at him like he had suddenly grown an extra head.

"There is a total solar eclipse occurring in three weeks," he continued. "It will track across the Midwest and the southeast. Trinity Cove is right in its path."

Of course it is, I thought. How could we have been so blind? The town had been promoting this for months now. We were expecting a bombardment of tourists flocking to the area for the show. It was the first one for Trinity in almost seventy years.

"That could do it," said Aunt Lena. "It's a rare event. The sun will be completely hidden for a few minutes."

"Long enough to hijack the eclipse," said Aunt Vivian. "If it can be done, that's when Mallis and his Warlock will make the move."

"Jesus," I said. "The town will be packed with tourists wanting to see the total eclipse. It will be close to chaos."

"It will be more than that," said Aunt Lena. "It will be a feeding frenzy for Mallis and any other vampires that he invites to the party. And believe me...there will be a party. A warping of nature of this magnitude will be like ringing the dinner bell at an all-you-can-eat buffet."

"So that explains why he didn't kill you," said Cody. "He needs you to power this spell, so he had to keep you alive until the eclipse. But why me? Why wouldn't he just kill me?"

"Werewolves are the rarest of all the Shifters," said Aunt Vivian. "They are very powerful, and the natural alphas of

Shifter communities. My guess is that Mallis knows the Warlock will need protection until the spell is complete. Wolves would be the natural choice."

"They have been going around trying to recruit Shifters," I said. "They're building an army."

"The eclipse is a daytime event. That means that Mallis can't be active in the Warlock's defense, at least not until the spell is completed," said Aunt Vivian. "And probably after the spell, he will be weak. The Shifters will act as bodyguards during the chaos that follows the darkness."

"And he would want Cody because you are a wolf that would no longer need the Order's magic, or any magic, to Shift. You would be an invaluable asset to them."

"Like that she-bitch that fought us," I added, ignoring the disapproving look Aunt Lena shot me.

"Exactly," said Aunt Vivian. "Not only would you be a powerful addition to his army, but you would be a natural leader of the Shifters that joined them. They knew you would never willingly join them, so that was why they sought to enslave your mind and spirit to their cause. It was a good thing your friends arrived when they did."

"I still feel like we are missing something," I said. "What does he really gain by doing this? I mean, it's not like everyone in the world isn't going to notice the sun not coming back out after an eclipse. It would bring a lot of unwanted attention to the supernatural community. Even an age-old vampire wouldn't want that kind of scrutiny; he has to have some other endgame in mind."

"Something you just said raises another question," said Cody. "Is this a localized event?"

"What do you mean?" asked Aunt Vivian.

"What he means is, when the eclipse happens over Trinity, it will have already occurred and be over in other parts of the country. If he freezes the dark here, it won't completely eliminate sunshine everywhere else. So there has to be more to his plan," I surmised.

Aunt Vivian shrugged. "Who can say how magic of this magnitude will work? It may not work at all…but I wouldn't want to bet on that."

"So this once again circles around to Hope's parents," I said. "Why kill them? Simple retribution for what I did?"

"I don't think so," said Aunt Vivian. "I think that the vampire is trying to take you out of the game mentally. He knew the effect this would have on you. The effect it is having on you."

Aunt Vivian gave a start, looking up with shock on her face.

"What is it?" I asked.

"Allie, where was Gar when this happened?" she said.

"At Isla Garner's house. She's the new veterinarian in town. He has been hanging out with her nephew for awhile now. Why?"

"But where does he usually stay when you have to leave him?" said Aunt Lena.

Oh, God. I could feel my palms break out in sweat. "At Hope's house."

"Jesus," said Cody. "You think they were after him?"

"Look at the effect killing your friend's parents had on you," said Aunt Lena. "Imagine what would have happened if it had been your brother. They are gambling that it would have taken you so far out of yourself mentally that recapturing you would have been a piece of cake. And you probably wouldn't have been able to put up much of a fight."

Goddamnit. How much more of this was I supposed to take? I had put my best friend in mortal danger, and now my brother, the light of my life, was becoming a target for these monsters. Just the thought of anything happening to Gar made me go weak in the knees. I could feel my spirit dying at just the thought.

I was numb as I stumbled into the living room and sank down on the couch, fully aware of the eyes that followed me.

Looking up at my aunts, steeling my resolve, I said, "Do you have any idea how this Leveling spell will work?"

They both shook their heads.

"However," said Aunt Vivian, "I think that now, armed with this new knowledge, we should once again approach the Witches' Council. They have access to the largest archives of lore and magic in the world."

Aunt Lena nodded her agreement. "There are those within the council that don't like the direction the council leaders are taking them. Maybe we can reach them, or at least reach them enough to get access to their archives and do a little research."

"How soon are you able to go back up there?" I asked. I hated the idea of them turning around getting on the road again.

"No driving this time," said Aunt Vivian. "We might be old, but we can still manage a teleportation spell—the kind we used to pluck you two and Gar out of the Falls that time before that Bear-Shifter made mincemeat of you all."

"Speaking of Gar," I said, "I need you take him with you." They both looked at me but did not hesitate to agree. "He is safer being away from me until this is over."

"What do you have in mind?" asked Cody.

"Simple," I replied. "I'm going to kill that Warlock... and then I'm going to do the same to that vampire. If it's a war they want, then flame on. I'm tired of running. I'm tired of being used and manipulated." I turned to my aunts and addressed them directly. "I'm going into your study and I'm going to absorb every ounce of mystical energy from every artifact and spellbook you have up there. And then I'm going to figure out how to kill a vampire and any other Godforsaken monster that gets in my way.

"But I can't do that if I have to worry about Gar. Get him out of here. Then I'm going to find Hope and make sure she never has to feel afraid again."

"And me?" said Cody.

"You're with me, big guy. We have to stop this Leveling before it can happen. I don't think I can take on the Warlock and a vampire and that she-wolf alone, let alone the other Shifters and human trash they may have gathered. I'll need help."

"I'm with you, you know that," he said.

"Still won't be enough. We need the other Shifters that are still in this. As well as Esmay."

I nodded. War was indeed coming to Trinity Cove. And we had mere weeks to level up for it.

Just then, Cody's phone rang. He looked at the screen before accepting the call. "Detective Walters, what's up?" The look on his face as he hung up told me something very unpleasant was going down.

"Cody, what is it?" I asked.

"A group of men just broke into the Veterinary Clinic. They took Dr. Garner."

Chapter Twenty-Two

"There were maybe four or five of them. They came in the back entrance and went right for her," Esmay was saying to Detective Walters when we arrived at the clinic. She was holding an icepack to the side of her face while a paramedic attended to her.

This was becoming all too familiar a sight: me arriving just in time to find someone I knew being Band-Aided back together, after having their life upended by a cruel act of violence. This time, I was sure my aunts were right.

These bastards were after Gar. At least this time they had decided to kidnap rather than murder the person they came across. Question was, how did they know he was supposed to be staying here?

"Esmay, what happened?" I asked, approaching her and the detective.

"We were in bed and there was a loud crash. Then, we heard footsteps on the stairs and a commotion in Jhamal's room. Suddenly, two men kicked in our bedroom door and charged at us. They were after Isla, and I went for them instead of trying to get to my blade. I got in a couple of good shots, but then another one must have hit me from behind. Everything started going dark after that."

"Any identifying marks on them?" asked Detective Walters. "Did they wear masks?"

"No, they were dressed in black with exposed faces. It just happened so fast, I can't be sure what they looked like."

"Esmay, where is Jhamal?" I asked.

"They took him and Isla, I believe. When I came to, they were both gone. His room was a mess; he must have put up a fight as well." She gave me a pointed look, one that spoke volumes between us. I had seen Jhamal in action in his lion form. There was no way he went down easy. Which begged the question: who—or what—was capable of taking out a Totem-Shifter?

"Is there anything at all you can tell us that might help us to identify the men that did this?" asked Detective Walters.

"I'm sorry. It all happened so fast." Again, she looked at me, her eyes fixed and hard. "They were fast—very fast."

So. Not human. Okay, I can work with that.

"Detective," another police officer called to Dana from the stairway and motioned for her.

"Excuse me," Detective Walters said. "I'll be back."

As soon as she stepped away, Esmay leaned in. "I know she knows what is going on, but I don't like her and I don't trust her." She grabbed my forearm and whispered quickly. "One of the men that hit me said something. He said to tell my little witch friend that she made a promise to come back and get someone. He said to tell you that that someone is still there, and now they have upped the ante by taking away the doctor who 'patches everyone up.'"

"Shit!" I said. Again, if they did anything to my friends,

it would be on my head. "Don't worry, Esmay. Nothing is going to happen to her or Jhamal. I promise you." Hollow words, but I hoped that I conveyed enough conviction that she believed in me.

"You know it's a trap, don't you?" Esmay said.

"Yeah. If I had a blind grandmother, she'd be able to see this one coming."

"So when do we leave?"

"What? Esmay, no. This is my fault and my fight. I'm not putting anyone else in danger. I'm going alone."

"Like hell. I don't give a flying leap whose fault it is. These maniacs have my girlfriend and my nephew. If hell is about to rain down on them, you'd better believe I'm going to be a part of it."

"A part of what?" said Detective Walters. She had walked back up behind us during our conversation, taking us both by surprise.

"Oh…the cleanup of the house. Allie was just offering to help with the mess left behind. As soon as we are able to touch stuff, I mean," said Esmay.

Dana arched a single eyebrow, clearing not buying any bullshit. "Indeed. Okay, well I suggest you find a place to stay for the next twenty-four hours. I want the boys from the crime lab to scour over every square inch of this place before the scene gets contaminated." She placed a hand on Esmay's shoulder and looked her in the eye. "I promise you, we are going to find the men who did this and bring Dr. Garner back home safely." Why was it so much more believable when she said it than when I had assured her practically the same thing?

"Allie, may I speak with you?" she said, stepping away from Esmay. I followed her to the front of the office space, near Esmay's reception desk. "Okay, what the fuck is going on around here? Your friend obviously knows something that might help us find whoever or whatever did this. Why is she not cooperating?"

As tired as I was, it didn't escape me that she had added "whatever" to the list of suspects. "Detective, trust me when I say that she has your best interest at heart if she keeps certain things from you—your best interest and your best health."

She drew back, raising that eyebrow in suspicion again. "Allie, what is it that you think I do? Why do you think that I was picked to come here and lead the investigation into whatever hell is going on in this town? Murder. Rape. Domestic abuse that would make your hair curl; that's the world I live in."

No more debating. Time was wasting and I was afraid she was on the brink of hauling me back to police headquarters again, so I took a chance. "This kidnapping is the work of the same forces that killed Hope's parents. Judging by what Esmay said, I think these were vampires. Not Shifters."

To her credit, Dana didn't flinch but instead seemed to let it all sink in. "Are Dr. Garner and her nephew dead?"

"I don't think so. The attackers gave Esmay a message to relay. I think they are using Isla and Jhamal as bait to get to me."

She sucked in a deep breath before speaking again. "So I take it that whatever they want with you can't be good, huh?"

"Depends. Is an apocalypse ever good?"

I looked away, unable to meet the stare that was aimed at me. I didn't know if she judging me on my words or my intent in that moment.

"I don't know if you mean that literally or metaphorically at this point," she said, "but I believe that you believe what you're saying. Either way, it sounds nasty."

"It is. There's a big bad with a serious hard-on for me, and it wants to use me as a mystical battery to power a spell that will literally bring about eternal darkness."

Detective Walters exhaled sharply and measured her next words carefully. "What do you need from me?"

"The same thing that Cody has been doing. I need you to run interference when needed. Keep the police out of this as much as possible. Give me a heads-up if it looks like they are getting too close to something they shouldn't—and by that, I mean any whisperings of vampires or Shifter activity."

"Allie. What killed your friend's parents?"

"Honestly? I'm not sure. But that was definitely the work of Shifters. Probably Bear or Wolf-Shifters, judging from the savagery of the attack." I looked at her and decided, what the hell; in for a penny, in for a pound. "I think they were after my brother Gar. He usually stays at Hope's place when I'm...busy."

"My God, that's terrible. Is he okay?"

"Yeah. He's safe now. I sent him away until all of this blows over."

"He is the boyfriend of the young man that was taken from here, right?"

I looked at her, unable to hide my surprise.

"Don't worry," she said, "what I know doesn't leave the vault." She tapped the side of her head with her finger. "A good detective makes it a point to learn everything about everyone remotely involved in a case they are investigating, Allie. And I am a very good detective." She smiled, and despite Esmay's misgivings, I couldn't help but return it. I liked this woman, and I had a feeling she would be able to provide us a lot of help moving forward. Or at least, that was my hope.

"Can I ask you something more personal?" she continued. I shrugged in response. At this point, what more damage could I do by revealing more? "What do you know about Cody's father?"

This caught me off guard. Of all the things she could have asked, I was not expecting this. "Not much. I know that he and Cody have a strained relationship. I met the man once, and to be honest, I don't care if I ever meet him again. Why?"

"Just curious. Back when he was in charge of the Trinity police department, he had dealings with my father."

That revelation shook me. She had said before that her father was involved in some shady business, and that he was a werewolf. Cody was a werewolf, and yet he had never intimated that his father was anything other than an upstanding servant of the people. But something here wasn't adding up; it all seemed too close to be coincidence.

"What kind of dealings?" I forced myself to ask.

"I'm not sure. Not yet, at least. But after my father was killed and I was going through his things, I found a couple of pictures of him with Cody's father. They looked like fishing or hunting pictures. The two of them seemed pretty chummy, which is what set my instincts off. Why would the chief of police of a small town, and my father—a known drug runner, mob enforcer and werewolf—be palling around?"

"Your father was killed?"

"Yep. Unsolved file. Officially, it was labeled 'a home invasion gone wrong.'"

"Seem to be a lot of those around here," I murmured, trying not to let my thoughts run wild. There was something that I couldn't get out of my mind since I had first met Detective Walters, and I figured now was as good a time as any to get it off my chest. "Detective, are you a Shifter?"

She regarded me briefly, cocking her head to one side. "No. I'm not. Like I said, my father was a werewolf, but it wasn't passed on to me. I have no idea how the gene... disease...whatever the fuck it is gets passed, but thankfully it seems to have skipped me. Would it have made you trust me more if I had said yes?"

"It would have depended on whether or not you had tried to rip my throat open like most wolves I've run into lately."

She nodded, the smile returning. "Fair enough."

"One last question, Detective: when did your father die?"

"Twenty-six years ago tomorrow. Why do you ask?"

"No reason. Just curious," I replied.

Twenty-six years ago. That was around the same time that my mother would have led the rebellion that destroyed all the wolves. It was also when Cody's father took him from that den of wolves, and decided to raise him as his own.

I believed in vampires, werewolves, Shifters, and hell, for all I knew, the Tooth Fairy and the Easter Bunny, but I sure as shit didn't believe in coincidences. Something wasn't adding up. But that could wait. First, I needed to rescue a couple of friends, and put the smack-down on a vampire and his little Warlock bitch.

Chapter Twenty-Three

I called a quick meeting at my house with Cody, Kendra and Esmay. We met outside on the top deck; despite the size of the house, I was feeling a little claustrophobic. Cody put on a pot of coffee as we began our little war council.

"I still say we hit them now," Esmay said. She was pacing back and forth, clenching and unclenching her fists. I could feel the waves of anger and despair rolling off her.

"Esmay," I said, "I know what you're feeling right now; believe me, I do. But if we rush in there and attack right now, then not only will Isla and Jhamal be dead, but probably us too."

"But it's almost dawn!" she exclaimed, pointing at the red glow gathering in the sky. "The vampire will be down and out; it's one less supernatural predator to worry about!"

"Esmay, we all know this is a trap, right?" I pleaded. "Going in right now is exactly what Mallis is expecting us to do. He probably wants us to attack. He will have countermeasures in place, I'm sure of it. Plus, how do we know that vampires have to sleep during the day? I saw that place…all the windows were boarded up and the interior is practically pitch-black in places. That has to be for a reason."

"I know. You're right," she said, plopping down on the lounger next to me. "It's just that…I mean…what if they're dead? Or dying as we speak?"

"They aren't," I said, placing one hand protectively on her knee. "Because then they would have no value. Mallis would not be able to use them as bartering chips for me. You said it yourself…those men told you that they want me to come and get them. That wouldn't be the case if they were dead."

"She's right," said Cody. He brought out a tray of coffee cups and we all grabbed one. "Of course, on the flip side, waiting gives them that much more time to prepare."

"True, but it also gives us time to get a plan together. Plus, we are all exhausted. We've been up nearly twenty-four hours, and Esmay probably twice that long. We can't go in there running on fumes."

"Like I'm going to be able to sleep…" Esmay muttered.

"You're going to try," I said. "We all are. Decaf, right, Cody?" I indicated the cups of steaming brown liquid he gave us.

"Yep. But the way I make it, you can't taste the difference," he replied proudly.

Yeah, right, I thought. Sure you can't. But I smiled sweetly at him, and nodded as I forced a swallow.

"So do we have a plan?" Kendra asked. She, too, had been pacing back and forth. Even in human form, her caged panther was showing.

I actually did have one. At least the bare bones of one. It was crazy, and might get one, or all of us, killed. But it was all I had. "First things first. Kendra, will we be able to count on the Shifter community?"

She nodded. "After you left, they had a meeting. The ones who walked out we knew were lost to us; but the rest, at least the ones capable of fighting, are all in. We have some new additions to our clan as well."

"The ones that you brought in from around town?" I really wanted to add "you mean the ones that I outed?" but I couldn't say it aloud.

"Yes. A couple of Bear-Shifters, and a cougar and an extremely large moose. These will help beef up our strength department. We'll need it if we're going up against more wolves."

"How do we know it's more wolves?" Cody asked.

"I asked Kendra to hang around Hope's house to see what she could find after all the cops left," I said.

"I definitely picked up the scent of Wolf-Shifters and more black magic," she said. She looked at Cody. "No offense, but wolves have a unique scent among Shifters. It's hard to mistake; it smells like old blood."

Cody blushed and shook his head. "No offense taken."

"That's good to know," I said, "about the scent of wolves I mean. Do all Shifters have a scent?"

"Yes," said Kendra. "It's a base smell of the animal they become, but it's layered with other unique touches that are infused with the magic that created them."

"What about vampires?" I said. "What do they smell like?"

Kendra wrinkled her nose. "When we were in the warehouse, I could smell the Shifters, the members of the Order, and their foul magic as well; but all of that was nearly suffocated by something I had never smelled before. Old corpse, sour milk, and rotted flesh. It was Mallis. Under their slick veneer, they are basically decomposing bodies. And he smells like something that has been dead for a very long time, but refuses to give up the ghost."

Well, that seems pleasant. But also helpful.

"Okay, so we arm the Shifters with an idea of what to look for—or in this case, smell for. I have a feeling that Mallis has already recruited more vampires. More than likely, they were the ones who attacked Esmay," I said.

"That would make sense," Esmay said. "They were very strong and fast. It would also explain how they were able to take Jhamal so easily. I didn't hear him roar, so I have no idea if he Shifted or not."

"If he didn't, then that could play into our hands as well. Kendra, does Jhamal smell like a Shifter?"

She shook her head. "No. That one smelled slightly of magic...but nothing like Shifter magic. To most, he would smell human; even in his Lion-Form he smelled like a human."

"So maybe they don't know what he is if he hasn't tried to escape," I added. "That could work to our advantage as well."

"Whatever you're planning, it sounds like it requires a lot of luck and what-ifs to succeed," said Esmay. She wasn't exactly wrong.

"There is one more element I need to bring into this mix," I said. All eyes turned to me and I took a deep breath. "For my plan to work, I need to ask Detective Walters for help."

I saw Esmay take a quick look at Cody. His inability to meet her gaze told her that I had already run this by him.

"Look, I know you said you don't trust her, but I do. And honestly, we need all the help we can get right now," I said. "Trusting her might be a risk, but right now it's a risk worth taking. For Isla and Jhamal, I say we need to do this."

She wasn't happy, but I could see reason and love overcoming Esmay's doubts. "Fine. But if she screws us, or fucks up, I won't hesitate to take her out if needed."

"She's a good cop," said Cody, "and from what I've heard, a good person. She wants to help."

"Fine," said Esmay. "If it helps get my family back, I'll do whatever."

"Kendra?" I said, looking over to where she was leaning on the deck rail, her attention focused out at the rolling trees before her.

"I'm in no matter what. I don't want any more of my people hurt by this Warlock."

"Okay," said Esmay. "Now that we have that out of the way, are you going to tell us this plan of yours?"

I took a deep breath and told them my entire plan. The looks on their faces mirrored the thoughts in my head.

"Well?" I asked.

"It sounds crazy," said Kendra.

"But crazy enough that it might actually work," added Cody.

Esmay looked from Cody to me and back to Cody again. "You sure you're willing to go through with this?"

Cody shrugged. "I trust Allie. If we are going to do this, we have to think—and act—outside the box."

"I hate that saying," said Esmay. "In business, it usually means someone just came up with an idea that was stupid enough to get them fired." She looked over at me and exhaled deeply. "But we can make this work. We have to."

"All right. Cody, go make the call to Walters," I said. "Esmay, you and Kendra go and get some sleep. There are two guest rooms downstairs that are already set up. I'd rather we not give that lunatic vamp any more targets to pick off. We all stay here until night. I'll double up the wards on the house just to be sure, but everyone under one roof seems the safest bet for now."

Maybe it was the weariness setting in, or they actually thought it was sound reasoning, but neither of them protested. Cody showed them to the lower level of the house, then went up to my bedroom to make his call. I busied myself with cleaning up the cups and emptying Cody's binge-water-slash-coffee down the drain. Just as I was putting everything away, Cody walked back into the kitchen.

"Okay, she's in," he said. Then he eyed the empty coffee pot that I was drying. "Oh, hey, did you finish off the coffee?"

"Sure did. It was too good to let just go to waste." The smile on his face made me feel okay about the little white lie I just told him. And that scared me. "No. No, Cody, I didn't. I would rather drink sewage than more of that. I'm just not a decaf kinda girl."

He side-eyed me, and then broke out in laughter. After a moment I laughed with him, enjoying just letting go and reveling in my feelings for the man I was falling in love with. He walked over to me and swept me into his embrace, bringing his mouth down to meet mine. I tried to stifle the small moan that escaped from deep within me, but my body refused to hide how much I wanted him. I turned my face to the side and buried it in his chest, taking in his strong, earthy aroma.

"I'm scared," I whispered.

He took my chin in his hand and raised my face to his. "Me too. But I believe in us. And together, we are more than a match for whatever this son-of-a-bitch vampire or Warlock can throw at us."

"Yes. Together," I whispered.

"Together," he said, before kissing me deeply again. This time I gave in completely to the heat and hardness that pressed against me. I bit lightly at his darting tongue before surrendering to the passion he had stoked within me.

Some time later, the chill of the kitchen floor brought us both back to reality. I must have dozed lightly because the next thing I was aware of was a hitch in my back and the tiny butterfly kisses with which Cody was nudging me awake.

"What time is it?" I groaned, suddenly aware that we had fallen asleep together, butt naked on the floor. I prayed that none of my houseguests had ventured upstairs for a drink.

"Not late," he said. "Time for a shower and a proper bit of sleep."

I stretched and let him lead me to my bath, where we both stepped under the hot water together. I kissed his shoulders and chest as he lathered my hair. The fading scars left over from his interrogation were barely noticeable under my touch as I traced them with a feather touch.

"Will it hurt much?" he asked.

"Yes." I was done with white lies.

Chapter Twenty-Four

At a half past seven, we left the house and piled into the back of Esmay's Navigator.

"Is it bad?" I asked Cody, turning to peer over the backseat to where he lay on his side. He was racked with pain, and it broke my heart to see him like that.

"On a scale of one to ten, it's about a fifty," he moaned through gritted teeth. He clutched his sides and rolled back and forth. Sweat poured off of him and I could hear his teeth gnashing together in an effort to stop the pain that rolled through his system.

"He looks really bad," said Kendra. "Are you sure this will work?"

"We'll find out," I said. Please, dear God, let this work.

I checked my phone for the time. We had forty-five minutes to get to the warehouse before sunset. I could only hope that Cody could last that long. I was about to place my phone back in my jacket pocket when it dinged once, the screen lighting up. The text was from Detective Walters and all it said was "IN PLACE." Good.

"Okay, Dana and the rest of the Shifters are in place. The rest is up to us for now," I said. Just then, Cody gasped, burying his face in his hands in an effort to stifle his screams. "Hold on, lover. Almost over."

"You should have gagged me," he moaned. "I refuse to scream like a little girl, but goddamn, this hurts."

I could feel the big SUV speed up as Esmay pressed hard on the accelerator. We tore out of the town limits and headed right for the warehouse on the outskirts of Queen City. I wanted more than anything to reach out with my magic and soothe the pain that coursed through my lover's body, but I knew that doing so would defeat the purpose of what we were about to attempt. In order for it to work, it had to be believable.

And that meant the pain had to be real.

"Five minutes," said Esmay.

"You two ready?" I asked.

My companions nodded in response. I could see Esmay reach over and grasp the hilt of her rapier, the feel of the leather scabbard an obvious balm to her rattled nerves. While she might not have liked the idea of waiting, she had slept soundly for a few hours, but I could tell from the strain on her face that she could have used a few more. She didn't say it, but I could read the fear on her face—not the fear of what might happen to her, but fear that we might be too late to save Isla.

Kendra sat calmly, her steely demeanor coiled tightly, ready to explode in a blast of action when needed.

I grabbed my phone and stabbed at the screen, sending a quick message to the detective. Meanwhile, Esmay eased the car off the road and into a stand of trees and bushes that would hopefully keep it concealed until we returned.

If we returned. No. Fuck that. When we returned.

Enter The Wolf

We jumped out of the Navigator and Esmay slipped her blade obliquely across her back. "You sure the spell you put on this will work?"

"In theory it will," I said. "The transmutation spell that turned the blade from lightweight steel to razor-sharp silver should be proof against the Shifters. Plus, it's even lighter than it was before, which should help you in the speed department."

"How can it be lighter if it's silver?" Esmay said in dismay.

I winked at her and smiled. "Magic."

The truck suddenly rocked violently next to us, and a low, rumbling growl echoed from the back. Esmay instinctively grasped the hilt of her blade and I could see Kendra's talon-like claws appear almost instantly. I waved them both off and tentatively approached the back of the truck. I placed one ear next to the back gate, listening carefully, but could not hear anything else coming from the vehicle.

"Cody, babe, are you keeping it together?" I asked, placing one hand on the back lift. The only answer I got was the sudden explosion of sound as the back door was kicked violently outward, knocking me to the ground.

Before I could recover, Cody was on top of me, and the full weight of his hybrid form threatened to crush my ribcage. He lowered his face to mine, fangs inches from my flesh, and growled menacingly. Then he reared back, howled loudly at the night sky, and in a flash wrapped one impossibly strong hand around my throat.

The next sensation I was aware of was being dragged

backward, the heels of my boots trenching through the dirt and gravel.

I was disoriented, and it took me a moment to realize that I was slumped in a sitting position, my head sagging onto my chest. A powerful hand had a hold on the collar of my jacket and I was being pulled along roughly behind someone.

Cody.

My face burned in pain and the soreness in my neck made me wince when I tried to turn and look at him. I tried to speak, but my throat was so raw and sore that I could do little more than squeak. The growl I got in response told me talking, even if I could, would be off the menu. Just moving my mouth made me taste something thick and bitter. I spit and tasted blood. Running my tongue over my lips, I could feel that the top one was split on the right side. The left side of my face felt swollen and strangely out of place.

That would explain why I couldn't see out of my left eye. It felt like it was glued shut. I tried to struggle in his grasp, and all that elicited was an explosion of red-hot pain in my ribcage. I felt like I had been kicked in the midsection by a mule.

Jesus. Did he kick me?

God, if I was in this bad shape, what had happened to Essay and Kendra? I pushed that thought out of my head as I felt the ground beneath me give way to asphalt. I could feel my jeans ripping, but was powerless to do anything. My head hurt too much to keep my good eye open, and my arms felt like lead. That was when I realized my wrists were bound in front of me, tied together by what felt like a length of electrical cord.

"Hey! Stop right there!" someone yelled from in front of us. I heard the distinctive click of the safety being removed from a handgun, and what sounded like a shotgun being chambered.

The hand that held an iron grip on my coat collar released me, and my useless body thudded backward onto the ground. I heard Cody roar in defiance, and sensed him leaping away from me. I couldn't move, not even enough to roll over to see what was happening, but I could hear the sudden swoosh of air being displaced by the powerful swipe of Cody's claws, followed by the sickening tearing sound of cloth, flesh and muscle. There was a muffled scream cut short by a terrible, wet, gurgling sound, and another thud.

Then, as if nothing happened, I felt Cody's incredibly large paw grab onto my collar and continue dragging me forward—only this time, I could smell a nauseatingly sweet scent coming off his claws. I struggled in vain, but to no avail.

I ceased trying to free myself when we both came to a stop. Only this time, he didn't drop me, and I heard the low rumble of Cody's warning growl escape his chest.

"Well, well...what have we here?" I heard someone ask. There were several more clicks of what I assumed were guns being leveled at us. "Looks like someone is lost."

"Kill it!" I heard someone else shout. "Did you see what it did to Petey? Fucking gutted him like a fish!"

There was a murmur that went through what I assumed was a gathering of guards in front of us. I twisted my head enough that I could make out the front entrance to the warehouse through my blurry vision. Couldn't see faces, but could definitely see jeans and combat boots lining the front of the entrance. Human guards.

"No," said another voice, cutting through the mounting tension. "Not this one. The master will want to see this one." Silence fell over them, and my heart jumped as I felt the soothing touch of magic flicking over my battered body. I reached for it, like a drowning victim grasping at a thrown lifeline, but then it was gone, pulled away from me, and the suffocating waves of pain once again crash over me, threatening to overpower my senses.

Cody grabbed me up yet again and I felt myself being hauled roughly up a flight of cement stairs to the warehouse landing. The change in atmosphere as we passed through the entryway into the climate-controlled cavernous space washed over me. I was aware that someone was walking with us down the long hallway, but trying to see in the fluorescent lighting was making me nauseous. The last thing I needed right now was to throw up; I could only imagine the pain that would bring.

I sensed that whoever was with us was the same person that had wielded the magic at the entry to the warehouse. As brief as it had been, I had been able to analyze the signature of the magic, even through the pain flaring inside me. It felt foreign—not to me, but to the person that was trying to use it. That meant that they weren't a witch. Most likely, it was a member of the Order, which would explain why they weren't freaked out by the presence of Werewolf Cody.

"Wait here," came the voice from beside us. Again, I felt another wave of magic flowing in our direction. It wasn't aimed at me; it was meant for Cody. Probably to keep him a little more docile, I figured.

I heard a door open and then shut, and a few more muffled words exchanged between a couple of parties. Almost immediately, the door opened again and we were surrounded by footsteps.

"So, it's true," said someone that I did recognize. It was the Warlock, and he was standing to my side. He walked around my body until he was in front of me. There, he squatted down until we were face to face. He reached out and cupped my chin in one hand, turning my head from side to side so that he could assess the damage that had been done to me. I heard him "tsk-tsk" a couple of times before he stood up and addressed Cody.

"Bring her in," he said. "This should prove most interesting indeed."

At this point, I stopped struggling, and let Cody haul me in like a useless sack of potatoes. He dropped me unceremoniously onto an area rug. I managed to roll partially onto my side—the one that was racked with horrible pain, but not excruciating pain. I coughed, and spit blood onto the carpet. There, that will show them.

"Well, well," said Mallis. "What have we here?"

"It appears that our attempt to subjugate the wolf, though not entirely successful, was not without its benefits," said the Warlock.

"I thought you said they extracted him before the sigils could be completed?" said Mallis.

"They did. We have never had the ritual interrupted before, so these are uncharted waters. Judging by the look of him, I would say that the spells worked their way into his system on some level. He's obviously been driven mad with the pain...he's practically rabid."

"And you think that pain drove him to come here?"

"Yes. The first thing the sigils and the magic do is indoctrinate the Shifter to return to its master. Even though its subjugation was not complete, it was still conditioned to return home, if you will."

"But what about her?" Mallis asked. "Why would it bring her here?"

"Now that, I'm not sure about," replied the Warlock. "It

could be that if he is now aligned with you, he sensed her as an enemy. Perhaps she tried to stop him from leaving… or…"

"Or what?" asked Mallis.

"Or perhaps the little witch tried to reverse the sigils and burn them out of him. She wouldn't have the experience to do that…so it may be what triggered his pain response and driven him here. He would have brought her along on instinct, the way a cat brings its owner a bird or mouse it has captured. A gift for you."

I could almost feel Mallis frowning. "Perhaps. And you are sure about her magic?"

"Yes, Master. She was beaten so badly that I doubt she could light a candle if she had to. The revelation spells show that she is barely conscious, and that any energies over which she has control are directed at the basic task of staying alive. She is ripe for a mystical harvest of her power."

"Still, I want to make certain," said Mallis. I could hear him turn and walk away. "First, take the werewolf upstairs and place him with the child. I want them both re-sigiled and locked. Then, let Shira at this one. I trust her nose for magic more than I do your spells."

Chapter Twenty-Five

I can't begin to explain how afraid and uncomfortable I was. Knowing that Cody had been removed from my side was scary enough; but seeing a gigantic she-wolf lumbering toward me—one that had recently tried to bite my face off—was enough to send my fight-or-flight receptors into overdrive.

Stay calm. You knew something like this was bound to happen.

Shira was in full wolf form when she moved next to me and began sniffing. I curled myself into the fetal position and tried to cover my face with my hands, but to no avail. The cord with which I was bound wouldn't allow me to adequately shield myself. I reached for my magic, but the throbbing in my head and how much it hurt just to draw breath curtailed even that.

The she-wolf leaned in close, and I could hear the great huffs of air as she inhaled and exhaled sharply. She bared her fangs with each forceful breath and growled slightly in my ear. I could only cringe when she unfurled her long tongue and licked the side of my face, before loping away to her master's side. There, she rose up onto her hind legs, shifting at the same time, until she stood fully erect next to the vampire.

"She's battered pretty good," Shira said. "Busted ribs, hairline fractures in one wrist, torn cartilage in her knee, separated shoulder blade, bruised kidney and...I do believe I smelled a little internal bleeding. He beat her up pretty good."

Bitch. I could practically smell the smug little smile coming off her.

"But she isn't using magic," said Mallis. "Why is that?"

"She is healing quick for a human," replied Shira. "I'm betting that whatever energy she didn't expend trying to heal her boyfriend, she is using to heal herself now."

"Interesting," said Mallis. "I believe my little Warlock to be correct...she is ripe for harvesting."

"Shall I have her taken to the holding cell with the other witch?" asked the Warlock.

"No," said Mallis. "I want to watch the spirit drain from this one as her mystical life force is collected. Bring the orbs here and draw her energies out before she regains sufficient power to throw up any type of defenses." He studied me again. I managed to give him my most defiant face. I tried to muster the strength to spit a mouthful of blood at him, but thought better of it at the last moment: might not be the wisest move to spit blood at a vampire. His lips split away from pearly fangs in a horrible mimic of a human smile. "Still a bit of fight left in you, I see." He turned to the Warlock. "Bring the orb that we have already filled with the essence of one of her fellow witches. I want her to see what she is in for."

Bingo.

I sensed the Warlock hesitate, but then he turned and barked an order at the flunky that had brought us into the warehouse. Flunky nodded and rushed out of the room.

"How long before her mate is completely back in the fold?" asked Mallis.

"His pain has driven him near to the point of madness. Remaking his mind will be part of the process if we are able to reach him. But even so, it shouldn't take more than a couple of hours until he is fully under your yoke."

"Good," replied Mallis. "He will make a fine addition to the ranks. Between him and Shira, we will raise a new army of wolves, ones that are free from the taint of magic." The Warlock was smart enough not to bristle at that last remark. I decided to throw a little gas on that burn and see what would happen.

"Tainted?" I wheezed. "Did he just call you dirty? 'Cause that's what it sounded like to me. Guess I see where Warlocks and vampires stand in the hierarchy of shit-bags."

The Warlock rushed to my side. "What's that supposed to mean? Coming from someone who will soon be little more than a living battery, it doesn't carry much weight."

"Like you don't mean much to him? You are beneath him, you know. He knows it. I sure as shit know it."

I expected a boot to the midsection for that, but thankfully it didn't come. The bitch-slap across the face, however, did. I laughed, spitting blood. "Wow...and to thank someone as weak as you defeated my mom." I saw him draw back a fist, and I clenched in preparation for the blow that didn't come.

"Enough," said Mallis. "Once you have her tethered and drained, you can do as you please with her husk. But for now, I don't want her beaten to death, and all that lovely magic leaked away into the ether."

He backed away, his eyes blazing with hatred. My face burned from his slap, but it was worth the hit to gain a little knowledge. He had attacked me physically, not mystically. This meant we must be in another of the dampening rooms, like the one from our first encounter. No magic was flowing inside these four walls.

I concentrated on trying to clear my vision. That slap, bitch-ass move it may have been, had still aggravated my swollen eye. Everything was blurry through my tears, but I could make out their flunky returning to the room, carrying a wooden box that was a little bigger than a shoebox. He opened it, and presented it to the Warlock.

The Warlock sat the box on a small table on the far side of the room, then reached inside to withdraw two globes, each about five inches in diameter. They reminded me of snow globes, and he carried them over to Mallis to inspect. But instead of a Burl Ives Christmas snowman with tiny shite flakes flying around it, they were murky and ethereal. One was filled with dots of light in various colors that bounced around inside the containment; the other was murky and dark with swirling tendrils of what looked like black smoke coalescing within.

The fact that Shira seemed to shrink back from the globes wasn't lost on me. And to be honest, the closer Mallis came to me, the more every instinct I had screamed at me to run from the packages.

"They are called Obsidian Spheres," he said, smiling gleefully at my obvious discomfort. "These little beauties are what collect the magical essence of you witches, and hold it for the Warlocks to use as they see fit. This one—" he held up the one with the brightly lit colors swirling around "—contains the energies of the witch you left behind a couple of days ago. She wasn't much—hardly enough to power the

Seeker spells used to track your friends. But beggars can't be choosers." He shrugged nonchalantly. "But this one..." He held up the darker globe. "This one has been created with a very specific purpose in mind. Can you guess what it will hold?" He looked at me and licked his lips lasciviously.

I've never wanted to punch a bastard right in the mouth more than I did right at that moment.

"And I believe that once we have the power of a Reliquary witch added to all that we have collected, we should have more than enough magic to power the Leveling—correct, my friend?" He turned and looked at the Warlock, who now stood off to one side. The Warlock only nodded and narrowed his eyes at me. I was unable to tear my gaze away from the spheres. Even with magic being dampened here, I could feel nothing but darkness and black magic coming off the shores in waves.

Where the hell did a vampire and a Warlock get something like this? Was this how Warlocks had been siphoning the powers off witches all along? I had read accounts of this, my aunts had told me about it as well, but no one seemed to know exactly how the power of a witch was stored and converted by a Warlock. I had always assumed they ingested the power inside themselves...but maybe that was wrong.

You know what they say about those who assume, don't you, Allie?

Mallis handed the globe over to the Warlock and sneered in his face. "Do it."

I could sense the hesitation in the Warlock as he glanced around the room. There was only Shira and the flunky present, but for some reason the Warlock seemed uneasy at the order. And it was an order, not a request; that much was certain.

That was when I noticed two shadows detach themselves from the far corners of the wall where the light did not reach. Both shadows glided into view, revealing themselves to be tall, lithe figures draped in hooded black cloaks.

Vampires.

Of course. They did love their drama.

They stood perfectly still, no doubt awaiting Mallis's orders. Whether they were there as guards or enforcers was anyone's guess. Had they been in the room all this time? Were there more of them? They had moved so quietly that I was certain even Cody's ears would not have picked them up. This definitely made things more interesting.

"Is there a problem?" Mallis asked. His tone made it plain that he was not accustomed to having to repeat himself.

"No problem, Master," said the Warlock. "It's just…not that I would question you…but this is typically done at the Sanctum, under more…controlled conditions."

"We do not have time for that," said Mallis. "We have one shot at the Leveling, and we don't have time for you to spend days upon days draining her. You've done this plenty of times before, so get on with it. Besides, I want to see her squirm as you suck the mystical life-blood from her. And then I want to watch her scream and beg for mercy as I let Shira have her physical body." His eyes grew blood-red as he spoke, and the husky tone that made its way into his voice creeped me out beyond the telling.

"Also," said the Warlock, "in order to do this here, it means we need to drop the wards that deaden magic in this cell."

"And?" said Mallis. "Are you worried that the witch might mount some sort of attack? Look at her. She can't even stand. Are you afraid that whatever meager magic this girl might call upon in her damaged state is more than you are capable of dealing with?" His arched eyebrow sealed the challenge, and the sudden swelling of the Warlock's chest punctuated his acceptance.

"She is severely injured," said the Warlock, "and she may not even survive the draining."

"So long as we have what we need, I really don't care," replied Mallis, stepping back.

"Very well," said the Warlock, nodding his head in agreement. Mallis took a few steps back as the Warlock raised his arms and locked his fingers together overhead. Then, closing his eyes, he breathed forth an incantation and pulled his hands apart, waving his arms in opposite directions. There was an audible pop as the wards that prevented magic came down.

That was all I needed.

"Now!" I said into the air, sending the word magically to my friends who had been waiting outside.

Chapter Twenty-Six

It was a variation of a glimmer spell I had cast. Glimmer, or "glamour" in some circles, is used by witches to alter the appearance of something—usually themselves, in order to appear younger or more desirable. It is basically illusion magic meant to deceive those around them.

But the spell I cast went far deeper than what met the eye. This was the 3-D printer of glimmers. I cast the spell deep, rather than just sending it wafting across the surface. I knew that I not only had to fool Mallis's magical adepts like the Warlock and the members of the Fell, but I also had to fool Shira. If a normal dog can be trained to sniff out tumors and impending seizures, then I could only imagine how sensitive a werewolf's nose might be. I had to make things look more than real; they had to be real.

Of course, the pain I felt was nothing compared to what I had had to inflict on Cody. I could feel the path of his scars when we were in the shower. He was healing quickly, which was one reason that we had to act quicker than I might have liked. If he had healed completely, I would not have been able to recreate the path of the sigils that had been cut into him. As it was, I will never forget the sound he made when I willed them to reopen and flooded them with magic to recreate the dark path that the Fell were burning into his very soul.

It must have felt like I was pouring liquid silver through his insides. It drove him to the brink of madness, but he had held on—until we got out of the car. Then, all hell had broken loose.

I hadn't accounted for Cody's accelerated healing. But the fact that he couldn't heal himself had caused the pain of the magical sigils to amplify. It drove him to shift, and the feral part of his brain took over completely. For a second, when he was on top of me outside the car, I thought he was going to kill me.

Esmay had hit him over the head with a tire iron and that seemed to jostle him back to normality long enough for me to work some magic into him and force him to remember who he was. It was tricky, though, and I could feel his hold on reality slipping. Part of him wanted to run, to just head off into the woods and live as a wolf. That part of him was buried deep—so deep that I doubted Human Cody was even aware of the impulse.

I tethered him to me with magic...reminding him of the times when he first shifted, and the touch of my magic both soothed and enraged his beast. But mostly soothed.

That was when I had finished the glimmer on myself, making it appear as if I'd been beaten to within an inch of my life. Then I had let Esmay bind my wrists, before she headed off to meet Detective Walters and the rest of the Shifters that Kendra had convinced to join us. They were gathered at an old construction site that flanked the warehouse and were waiting on my signal.

I hadn't counted on them removing Cody from my sight, and I could only pray that he had held on long enough to hear my signal.

With the wards down, I wanted to reach out to him, reassess our bond and remove the glimmer that was causing him so much pain. But I didn't dare. I had to focus on my target, the vampire that was behind all of this, standing mere feet away from me.

At the same time, gunfire and screams broke out from somewhere outside of the warehouse, followed by an incredibly loud roar that I recognized as Kendra. She was leading the Shifter brigade in their charge on the building. I heard return fire coming from outside the warehouse, and knew it had to be Detective Walters entering the battle.

Fangs and claws were great, but sometimes a situation called for good old-fashioned gunfire.

As soon as I sent the signal out, I dropped the glimmer that had fooled them all and focused my power on the "cord" that bound my wrists. The glimmer fell away from it as well, revealing my silver belt that had been wrapped around my hands. I breathed fiery magic onto the slender belt, willing it to life. It glowed blue-white, imbued with all the magic I could muster. I thrust my hands forward in the direction of Mallis and sent it pinwheeling through the air.

Let's see how long he gloats with no head. The literature might be shoddy on just what a vampire of his age was capable of, but some things were universal: cut off the head and the body dies.

I hoped.

Unfortunately, I wouldn't have the opportunity to test that theory. At the last possible second, moving like liquid light, Shira appeared between my belt and the intended target's neck. She managed to get one hybrid paw up in front of her, jamming it between my improvised bolo and her neck. Still, the power of the line sizzled as it made contact, wrapping itself around her limb and neck, knocking her backward while she howled in pain.

Mallis glared at me, baring his fangs and hissing like a cobra. I guess the movies got that part right. Who knew he would actually hiss?

Before I could react, more members of the Fell flooded into the room. Chanting in unison, they charged at me.

Not this time, boys. I had come prepared for this.

I concentrated, summoning magic in the form of ball lightning, and hurled it at the first attacker, the same guy that had escorted us into the room. His scream was snuffed out in his throat as the heat of my mystic attack shorted out his internal respiratory system, before arching in leaps and bounds to his fellow flunkies. I smiled as they fell into a smoking heap on the floor.

There was another crash and more roars from upstairs, and I could actually feel the warehouse foundation shake in response. But I still had no time to worry about that. I had a vampire to kill.

I looked over to where Shira had fallen, and saw that she was writhing on the floor. Blood was pouring from her paw as the belt fought to constrict it tighter. I was tempted to call it back, but I knew taking her out would be almost as useful as taking out Mallis himself. Instead, I looked around for another object to use as a weapon, fully aware that at any second I might feel those fangs of his digging into my throat.

My eyes lit on the one thing in the room I thought I could maybe make use of, but as I started to run toward it, I felt the searing bite of magic. Something red and crackling wrapped itself around me, stopping me in my tracks. It felt like my spine had been dunked in freezing water and ripped out of my body.

I turned, still held fast by the shimmering black magic, to see the Warlock standing with his arms outstretched, hands glowing with red power. He closed his fists, and I could feel the mystic noose tightening around me. I resisted the spell, concentrating my own magic into that which was binding me. I felt the Warlock redouble his efforts, chanting a spell that caused the red bands to squeeze even harder as I struggled.

In desperation, I reached out for the only weapon I knew I could use: my belt. I heard Shira scream as the belt broke through her paw; it would have snapped her neck if I hadn't called it to my side. I caught the glowing chain in one hand and whipped it down across the energy that held me. There was a loud crackle as sparks of magical light filled the air on impact. I could feel the Warlock shudder as I fought back, spurring me on to pour more blue light into my silver chain.

I swung it over my head and whirled it in his direction. He redirected his red magic to form a shield in front of him, to take the brunt of the hit. Unlike Shira, he did not possess the dense musculature and bone density of a Shifter to thwart the chain. It would have had no problem shearing through his flesh given the chance.

The distraction, small as it was, gave me the chance to break free of the red binding spell, and hurl myself at the object of my original desire: the Obsidian Spheres. I called to the glowing orb to summon it to my hand at the same time that Malls launched himself at me.

The Sphere was in my hand almost instantaneously, but the Vampire nearly matched its speed. As soon as I made contact with the Sphere, I felt the magic stored within it blaze to life. Light flared outward into my immediate vicinity and magic coursed through me. Time slowed down around me, or at least it felt that way. Mallis, close as he was, suddenly seemed frozen in midair, nails and fangs bared and aimed at my throat. He was inches from my neck, and yet thanks to my magic, I was able to dodge the deathblow.

I stepped away from him, still in awe at how slowly he appeared to be moving through the air. I looked over at the Warlock, and he too was moving slowly—even moreso than Mallis, as he did not possess the vampire's preternatural speed.

Just as suddenly as it happened, I could feel the magic waning and the vampire was beginning to pivot in misstep, adjusting his stride to once again turn and reach for me. The look in his eyes told me he meant business, and as soon as the spell ended, so too would my life.

So I did the only thing I could think of; I smashed the Sphere into Mallis's face with all the strength I could muster. The orb shattered into a million pieces, releasing tendrils of light in willowy wisps around the creature's face. I reached out with my magic, just as the spell broke, and gathered those vaporous bits of eldritch energy, praying that whoever that power had once belonged to would forgive me for using it this way.

I shaped the magic, added my own to it, and willed it into the vampire. I watched as it entered into his mouth, eyes and ears. Any opening on Mallis's body was fair game as I forced the power into him. He dropped to his knees, his body contorting like the girl's from The Exorcist. That movie scares the shit out of me even to this day, but it was nothing compared to the horrible crunching and breaking sounds coming from Mallis as I willed the magic to pull him into a hundred different directions at once.

I was so focused on the vampire that I didn't see the Warlock coming. The spell that had frozen him had worn off, and he was coming at me from the side with a nasty black dagger. I threw up a shield with one hand while struggling to maintain my power over the vampire.

The Warlock's first strike hit my shield point first, and I could see him beginning to chant again, trying to break through my shield so that he could press the dagger home. I was sweating. No way I was keeping this up against the both of them much longer. To make matters worse, I saw Shira start to move out of the corner of my eye. She had dragged herself up from the floor, her eyes filled with hate, as she examined her amputated paw. Then she shifted and howled in my direction.

Shit. Well…I had given it my all. But I still wasn't going out like this. I'd draw all the magic I could into me in one last attempt at blowing everyone around me into smithereens, if need be. I dropped to one knee, buckling under the strain of keeping up my power at this level. But before I could go all suicide-magic-bomber, another form burst into the room.

It was Esmay, her silver rapier slicing through the air. She dove at the Warlock, driving the sole of her boot into his side in a vicious kick that sent him scrambling one way and his dagger flying the other.

I could breathe again, but before I could renew my attack on the vampire, Shira leapt at me, slamming her full wolf form into my shields. The impact caused me to lose my grip on the vampire as I struggled to defend myself against the werewolf. I summoned power into my fist, ready to blast her full in the face as she circled around a second time to pounce. But before I could fire at her, I felt the sizzling heat of a bullet flying past me to lodge itself in Shira's side.

The large wolf barely flinched as she turned to bare her fangs at Detective Walters.

She crouched, preparing to leap, as the detective fired another round into her flank. It didn't even slow Shira down as she bounded into the air, her jaws opening wide to rip Dana apart. She didn't make it, however. A blurry shape struck her in mid-leap, sending her crashing and skidding across the concrete floor. The body of one of the guards, mauled beyond recognition, clattered to a stop beside the large wolf.

Behind Detective Walters stood Kendra in full panther form, another guard held in her massive jaws. She shook him like an oversized ragdoll before tossing him aside as well. She stalked toward Shira, a rolling growl vibrating from her powerful chest.

After them, a great lion entered the room with a roar that shook the rafters. There were two wolves on Jhamal, each trying to land a death bite on his throat, as they all rolled into the room, teeth gnashing, claws tearing into flesh. Jhamal's golden mane was red with blood and his face was coated in gore. Given Jhamal's appearance, the wolves weren't as bloodied as you would think. That told me he must have run into more than just this mangy pack. Good. The more damage he did, the fewer of them to fight our way through later.

I turned my attention back to Mallis, reaching for the magic I had left and intending to finish what I had started. He was nowhere to be seen. He had not fled through the door during the commotion, so he had to be in the room somewhere. He was vampire, I reasoned, so in my mind that made him like a ninja, meaning he would probably play in the shadows and take me by surprise.

I saw the barest movement flit through my peripheral vision, and I spun in time to catch of glimpse of him darting from one corner of the space to another. I ignored the shots ringing out as I raced across the room to where I thought he had gone. I held my magic in front of me, a glowing blue ball that would strike into the dark corners and erase his hiding spots. He was cornered, but then I heard something that made me stop in my tracks.

It was a howl and a roar, unlike anything I had ever heard in my life. It echoed with pain and rage, bouncing off the walls around me.

Cody.

I looked around to see that other Shifters had joined the fray. A large eagle had one of the guards pinned beneath its talons as it pecked mercilessly at his entrails. A Tiger-Shifter and a Bear-Shifter were rolling around, each seeking to land a killing blow on the other. I saw Jhamal flinging aside one of the werewolves, just as the other and Shira joined together to circle the great lion.

And then, just outside the door, I saw Cody. He was in his hybrid form, covered in blood, his face cut and damaged so badly that I wasn't sure he could see through all the blood pouring down into his eyes.

I forgot everything I should have done, and instead focused on the one thing I knew I needed to do.

I ran across the gore-splattered space and out into the hall. Cody was roaring at the two guards that advanced on him with guns, as well as the two members of the Fell that were trying to flank him, black daggers at the ready.

No time for niceties. I summoned as much magic as I could and cast it outward in a single horizontal blue band.

It hit all four assailants at once, mid-torso, and sliced them neatly in half. One minute they were standing, and the next minute, what remained of them sizzled and smoked as they fell to the floor.

I turned to face Cody and held my hands up, calling my magic back inside me.

"Cody, babe...it's me, Allie." He roared, baring his fangs in my direction. The sigils that I had magically re-carved into him were glowing silver and pulsed in the dim light in the corridor. "Cody, listen to me...you know me. You know I would never hurt you...this was all part of our plan, remember?" He stepped toward me, snapping his jaws together in a frightening chomping sound that caused my blood to run cold in my veins. His claws were still extended in my direction and they dripped red. "I need you to relax, okay? Let me help you."

I summoned my magic and sent a soothing pulse in his direction. He felt it and recoiled slightly. I had dropped the glimmer, but I needed to close the wounds created by the sigils, and that would require a little more of an invasive touch.

I stepped forward slowly, keeping my tone just above a whisper. "It's okay, I'm not going to hurt you. I need to help you remember, that's all." When I was close enough, I placed a single hand lightly on his chest. No magic...just human contact. "I swear, I'm not going to hurt you." He bared his fangs again and leaned forward, his jaws inches from my face. I could see his nose quivering as he breathed me in, trying to decide if I was friend or foe. Or food, judging from the way he was salivating.

"It's okay," I breathed, releasing a small pulse of magic. He trembled but didn't draw away. I looked him deep in the eyes as I recalled the sigil magic that was poisoning him, draining it away, and along with it, his anger and pain. "I love you, Cody," I whispered as I drew out the last of the magic, closing the wounds that were coursing through his cut flesh. "I love you."

I felt his hand on my back. His human hand. His features once again took on those of the man on whom I had come to rely more than anything else in this crazy world. "I love you," I said again, my eyes tearing up, "and I promise I will never do something like this to you again."

"Allie?" he whispered, taking my hand in his and looking down at me. "I..." He was cut off by the blurring form that suddenly appeared beside us.

With a single blow, Mallis sent Cody crashing into the far wall, and then he scooped me up in an embrace that I had no hope of breaking.

"How sweet," he said, before burying his fangs into my neck.

I felt a moment of pure shock, the kind that can only be felt when a creature from your darkest nightmares actually starts to eat you.

Then, blissfully, I felt nothing, as darkness rolled across my vision and sent me tumbling downward.

Chapter Twenty-Seven

I was aware of the smell of tea and bacon, and the soft down of my pillow under my head.

I opened my eyes, grateful for the soft tapered light that filtered through my closed blinds. The world came into focus in bits and pieces of color. It was like looking through a toy kaleidoscope, constantly turning it until settling on an image pleasing to the eye.

I tried to sit up, but felt a strong yet soothing hand press gently on my shoulder.

"Easy there," said Cody. "Don't try to get up just yet."

"Where am I?" I croaked, suddenly aware of the severe raspiness of my throat. "What happened?"

"It's okay. You're home." He turned toward the door to my room. "She's awake now," he called.

My aunts came strolling into the room, carrying a tray of tea and a breakfast plate between them. Gar filed in afterward, not hesitating to plop onto the bed next to me.

"Finally," Gar said playfully. "I didn't think you were ever going to wake up!"

"How long have I been out?" I asked, navigating through the cobwebs in my brain.

"Almost three days," said Aunt Vivian.

"What?" Now I sat up in earnest, shocked into awareness. "How is that possible? We were just at…" Then I remembered, and reached for my neck, feeling the bandage wrapped around it. I panicked and started clawing at the wrapping.

"Hey, hey…it's okay," said Cody, reaching out to gently grasp my hands. "Dr. Garner patched you up. She's in the guest room sleeping. She stayed up with you around the clock until she was certain you were out of the woods." He nodded to Gar, who then bounced off the bed and rushed from the room.

"Three days? What happened though? Where is everyone…"

"Everyone is fine. A few bumps and bruises, but nothing that won't heal," said Aunt Lena.

"When did you get back to town?" I asked.

"Cody called us that night." She didn't need to say what night. "We came back immediately."

"I thought…I thought we might have lost you," said Cody. "I couldn't imagine not having your family here."

Aunt Vivian reached over and squeezed Cody's hand in a manner that made me feel warm and relaxed at the same time. Just then, Gar bounded back into the room trailed by Isla Garner and Esmay.

Aunt Vivian and Aunt Lena stepped aside as Dr. Garner approached me, stethoscope in hand. "It's good to see you awake, Allie. How are you feeling?" She rubbed the chill off the stethoscope before placing it against my chest to listen to my breathing.

"I feel like I was hit by a bus. My head is killing me and

my throat is so raw…" I reached up again and felt the bandages. "Oh my God…he bit me!"

"Yes, he did," said Isla. "And he nearly drained you."

I swallowed hard, looking around the room at the somber faces staring back at me.

"Why didn't he finish me off?" I asked.

"Don't know," said Cody. "When I came to, you were lying in a puddle of blood. But Mallis was nowhere to be seen."

"What about the other witch that he had locked in one of those rooms? It was her magic that was inside that sphere —the magic I was able to draw on when I fought Mallis. Did you find her?"

"We didn't have time to sweep the entire space," said Esmay. "But I'm pretty sure there were no other hostages there other than Isla and Jhamal. If there was a witch, she was moved before we arrived or she was…" She didn't need to finish that sentence.

"We were winning," I said. "I remember that. We had them against the ropes. What happened after I went down?"

Esmay sighed and glanced at Cody before continuing. "Yes, we had the upper hand—until the Warlock called for reinforcements. A wave of Shifters attacked the warehouse, pouring in from the surrounding areas. They attacked, and that was when we started to realize we were seriously outmatched."

I looked around the room, a cold sweat starting to form across my back. "Where is Dana? Did she make it?"

"She did," Cody said. "She has a broken arm, but she'll mend. She fought hard. Her gun came in very handy."

"We were surrounded," said Esmay, "but the Shifters and the human followers of the Warlock seemed more intent on getting something...or someone...out of the warehouse."

"How do you know that for sure?" I asked.

"Because we are still alive," said Esmay. "Trust me, they could have killed us, but it was more like they were keeping us busy. And then, all at once, it was like a signal was given, and just as quickly they retreated."

"Maybe it was the girl," I said. "Maybe they hadn't completely drained her and needed to take her to wherever their next safe house might be."

"Maybe," said Esmay thoughtfully. "But if they needed a witch, why didn't they just take you?"

I didn't have an answer for her. I was just glad that we were all still around and in one piece.

"You need some rest, my dear," said Aunt Vivian. "We can continue this later."

"I've been resting for three days, Aunt Vivian. I need to move around some." I tried to get up but was overcome by a wave of nausea that forced me back onto the bed.

"Go slow," said Isla. "Like I said, it will take you awhile to recoup all the blood you lost."

"The blood," I said. "Am I...I mean will I..." I couldn't bring myself to finish the thought.

"Turn?" said Esmay. "No. Your blood samples appear completely normal. While we still don't know everything about vampirism, it appears that some sort of transfer of his blood into your system has to happen to create a change. He just drained you. Maybe he thought you would die from the amount he took; that's why he left you."

"If I've been out for three days, has there been any movement from the Fell or the Warlock? Any signs they are still active?"

"Nothing," said Cody. "They've gone to ground. Detective Walters ordered a sweep of the area, claiming possible domestic terrorism as grounds, yet she found no traces of where they went."

"I have to ask," said Esmay. "Why did you involve the detective? Was that wise?"

"Because," I replied, "she needed to see for herself what we are up against. She was determined to involve herself in this one way or the other, but she didn't really know what she was in for. Now she does. She will either help us, or she will leave us alone to handle this. Next move is up to her." A shadow crossed my mind as I remembered what she had said about her father's dealings with Cody's father...but I filed it away. That could wait.

"We rattled them," I said. "I almost had Mallis. We have to find them while we have the advantage."

"No," said Cody. "We don't have the advantage. They weren't kidding when they said they have raised an army."

I thought about it and shook my head. It didn't matter what they had. I was determined to stop this Leveling from happening, and that meant I had to be better prepared for the next time, the final time, I met that vampire.

"Aunt Vivan, Aunt Lena," I said, "I need you to take Gar and go. Mallis has shown that he won't hesitate to target my family, and I'll feel better knowing the three of you are safe and..."

The look that flashed through Aunt Lena's eyes caused me to stop mid-sentence. Her eyes clouded over and I could feel the swell of her magic tremble in the air.

"Allie Caine," she said, her voice hard and pointed, "don't even think about it. We should never have left you the first time. We may be old, and seriously out of practice when it comes to magic, but we are still witches. Maybe we aren't Reliquaries, but we are witches nonetheless. And furthermore, we are family. And we are not leaving your side again."

I felt a lump form in my throat as I looked over at Aunt Vivian and then Gar. Each reflected the same steely resolve that Aunt Lena had. I knew that arguing would be useless.

"Fine," I said. "But I need to get up. I have a lot to do."

"Just what do you have to do besides to get better?" said Aunt Vivian.

Now it was my turn to muster my resolve. "For starters, I need to go and visit my best friend and let her know that I made a mistake but that I love her as much as anyone in this room, and I'm not leaving her until we work things out. Then I have figure out how that Warlock steals our powers and seals them away in those spheres. Then we have just over a week to figure out how to stop a literal supernatural dark age from occurring. And finally...I need a spell that will kill a vampire once and for all."

No one spoke, but they all looked at me.

"We can't do it alone," said Esmay. "The Shifters that we still have on our side are no match for what Mallis has at his beck and call."

"I've been thinking about that," I said. I turned and looked at my aunts. "Tell me. What do you know about Otherkin and Totem-Shifters?"

Chapter Twenty-Eight

Three Days Prior: Mallis

"Well that was fun," said Mallis, striding across the massive master suite of the mansion in which he resided, far from the warehouse where he conducted business. He had raced through the city on foot, arriving back at the house well before his mate arrived, escorted by a team of werewolves and human guards.

"That was reckless," said the woman as she entered the room, her long cloak flowing behind her. "They barely got me out of there in time."

Mallis greeted her warmly, embracing her before bestowing a deep and loving kiss on her rose-red lips. "You were in no real danger. Despite what you said, I would have killed her before allowing her to face you."

"Are you sure she is still alive?"

"Yes. Granted, I was tempted to finish her, but her heart is strong. It was still pumping when I left her. She will be out of our hair for awhile, but she will live."

"Is she as strong as we hoped?"

"Stronger. I took the measure of her power, and I must say...it stung."

"Good," replied the woman, stroking the side of her lover's face gently. "With her raw power, we will not have a problem completing the spell. Did you get what we need?"

Mallis went over to the dresser and retrieved two objects. He held up the Obsidian Sphere and handed it to woman. "The sphere contains no magic from her. We did not get to drain her before her friends interrupted."

"No matter," she replied. "This sphere was in her presence while she worked her magic. A trace of it is all I need. And the other?"

Mallis smiled and extended his fangs. He held up a small test tube and gently bit one elongated incisor through the black rubber topper that sealed it. Then, like a snake being milked, he released a stream of blood into the container.

"Her blood," he said, handing it over to the woman. "Just as you asked for."

In the dark, the lady's eyes flashed black, and she smiled. "Yes. This will do."

"We will have to deal with her friends," said Mallis, "and her family. They are proving more resilient than we thought."

"Yes," she replied. "They are resilient. And stubborn. Just like Allie."

Mallis walked over and again swept her into his arms. He peppered her neck with kisses and whispered in her ear, "Stubborn indeed. Just like her mother." He pushed a strand of his lover's red hair back. "Are you certain you are ready to do this to your only daughter?"

Enter The Wolf

The lady laughed, deep and raspy, before throwing herself in her lover's arms. They sank to the bed, giving themselves fully to the heat of their lust.

Next in the Shifter Wars Series

vinci-books.com/returnofthewitch

Eternal darkness is on the horizon—and she's the only one who can stop it.

With the help of her loyal shifter clan and the Otherkin Totem Shifters she brings into the world, Allie must face Mallis's army of wolves and his deadly new weapon: a powerful witch summoned from the dark realms. Armed with courage and her newly claimed birthright, Allie takes her place at the centre of a supernatural war that will determine the fate of the world.

Turn the page for a free preview…

The Return of the Witch: Prologue

AN UNINVITED GUEST FOR DINNER

Admittedly, I was terrified.

It took every ounce of willpower I had not to summon my magic and throw it at the mess in front of me. Honestly, I didn't know what would happen if I did use magic. I had never tried it in a situation like this before. Resisting the urge, I wiped my brow and leaned in closer to look at the soft white peaks that were rising before me.

"Allie, are you sure you want to do this?" It was my Aunt Lena leaning in to whisper in my ear. "You have to be careful. One little mistake and it will be all over."

"You think I don't know that? Now back up, you're too close; you're making me doubt myself."

It was too late to stop now; I was all in.

I found myself holding my breath as I reached forward and turned off the stand mixer sitting on the kitchen counter. I eased the blade up and out of the bowl, marveling at the perfect stiff peaks of egg whites I had beaten. They clung to the blades with just the right consistency, and the soft yet firm waves inside the bowl looked like silky, frosty peaks that had frozen in time just as they crested.

Perfect. Now to get them folded into the orange base sauce I had cooked, and into the ramekins without overmixing them. The thought of ruining this was making me break out in a sweat. Christ, I hadn't felt this kind of pressure when fighting werewolves and vampires. That was a walk in the park compared to making a perfect orange soufflé with a Grand Marnier topping.

"Allie, are you sure about this?" Aunt Lena said, wringing her hands. "I mean, it's not too late to put in a peach pie. I bought a brand new tub of vanilla bean that will be perfect on it."

"No, Aunt Lena. This is my first big meal having Hope over since everything with her parents. It has to be perfect. She loves dessert and I intend to blow her out of the water with this one."

"Well, I'd say the main course certainly did that," Aunt Lena replied.

She was right, of course. For dinner I'd made grilled swordfish with provencal sauce. It was delicious, if I must say so myself. Combined with the grilled asparagus and endive salad with champagne vinaigrette, it had been the best meal I'd ever made, and Hope had been more than just a little impressed. But this would take the evening to a whole new level; this would send her into sensory overdrive.

If I could get it into the oven and it baked perfectly. Without collapsing. I'd die if it collapsed. And I was pretty sure that no magic spell in the world would fix this if I fucked it up. I could probably fix a fallen angel easier than I could a fallen soufflé.

Aunt Lena opened the oven door for me and I gingerly placed the mini ramekins into the lower third, praying they would rise just right, and not have burned tops. Exhaling, I turned to high-five my aunt before setting the timer for thirty minutes. Not that I trusted the timer; I would watch these bad boys like a hawk.

"Shall I offer everyone tea while we wait?" Aunt Lena asked.

"Thanks, but no. I think this calls for something little more special." I went to the large refrigerator and retrieved a bottle of pink Prosecco. "Tonight deserves a bit of bubbly, I think."

Aunt Lena's face lit up and she clapped her hands in glee. "Vivian will not approve, but I think you're right. I'll get the good glasses." She set about collecting six champagne glasses and arranging them on a serving tray, while I removed saucers from the cupboards on which to serve the little soufflé when they came out of the oven.

"What is that I smell?" said Hope, walking into the kitchen.

"Hey! It's a surprise! Go back outside. We'll be out in a few with some drinks before dessert," I said.

"Oh, you know I love me some dessert! What is it?" She attempted to peak into the oven, but a single glance from me caused her to throw her arms up in resignation and head back out onto the deck where we the table was set. I could hear laughter through the open French doors that led outside, and for a moment, I almost forgot the world of shit we were all in.

The tray full of glasses and bottle was a little wobbly in my hands as I made my way outside.

"Here, let me help," said Hope, taking some of the glasses and setting them on the outdoor coffee table that was positioned between a sofa and two chairs at one end of the deck.

"Yes! Champagne!" said my brother Gar, giving a small fist pump.

"No way," I said. I nodded at a second bottle on the tray. "That's for you and Jhamal. Sparkling cider."

He fake grumbled, but reached for the glasses nonetheless. He winked at me knowingly. We both knew it wouldn't be his first sip. I wiped the sweat from my palms on the back of my jeans, hoping no one noticed.

Hosting a dinner party in the midst of a war against a vampire with an army of werewolves and a Warlock at his disposal might not have been my best idea. But I needed to mend things with Hope. She was my best friend, and because of my actions, her parents had been horribly murdered. Okay, maybe it wasn't entirely my fault, but I certainly felt guilty.

No matter how I tried to spin it to myself, I kept thinking: what would have happened if I had never shown up with Cody at her house that first night? The night he shifted and we were attacked by members of the Order of the Fell. Had I never been at Hope's house, she would have never been on the Warlock's radar. And if she hadn't been on their radar, then maybe her parents would still be alive.

And our friendship wouldn't have taken the weird turn it had.

Harsh words had been spoken and feelings had been hurt. But Hope was more than a friend; she was as much a part of my family as my aunts and Gar. So I had visited her while she was in the hospital under evaluation after the death of her parents. We yelled. We cried. And ultimately, we forgave. Or rather, she forgave. Me? I mostly just groveled and offered words and my heart. In the end it was enough to get her talking to me again. But I knew better than anyone that some wounds can fester long after the skin has healed over them.

That was why I had demanded that she stay in the guest bedroom until she was ready to start thinking about what to do with her parents' house. Today was her first day after moving in, so I was determined to make it special. The dinner and the dessert were key comforts we had always bonded over, and the least I could do was make these memorable.

I hadn't invited my boyfriend Cody, and he understood why. While he had the best of intentions towards Hope, and I didn't doubt the love he had for me, he was still a werewolf —and werewolves had killed Hope's parents. No point in poking that bear again.

My aunts were onboard with her staying here, and I know Gar had no issues with it either. After what we had all been through in the last week, we all recognized the importance of family. No more lone wolves; this pack was staying together no matter what was thrown our way.

The bubbly was exactly what I needed. Light, fruity, and just the right amount of buzz-inducing, without being overpowering. Part of me was still focused on listening for the timer to go off, and it was all I could do to resist going back into the kitchen to peek into the oven and seeing what my little ramekins of goodness were doing.

"So Allie," said Gar, "it's been awfully quiet the last week. Do you think Mallis and company have moved on?"

The silence that fell over the deck was deafening. I wanted to frown at my brother, but he was looking at me with such earnestness that I felt my heart breaking. Jhamal placed one hand behind Gar's back and rubbed his shoulder comfortingly; I knew without asking that Gar was afraid for his boyfriend. Jhamal and his aunt had been kidnapped by the Warlock and Mallis to be used as bait—to get to me. By working together, my friends and I had managed to save everyone, but I was sure the thought of what could have happened was still very fresh in Gar's mind.

"This is a war, Gar," I said. "I don't think they just gathered their troops and went home. Something tells me they're biding their time."

"And what about us?" he replied. "I mean, what about you guys? What are you planning to do to stop him?"

"Gar," said Aunt Vivian, "now's not the time to discuss this."

"Well when is?" he replied. "Are we waiting for them to attack again? To kidnap or murder someone else we love?"

I sensed Hope flinch at that one and I gave Gar a look that shut him down.

"I'm sorry," he said, addressing Hope. "I didn't mean that to come out like it did."

"It's okay, Gar," Hope said. "I know what you mean. For what it's worth, Allie, I'd like to know what the next steps are going to be as well. I've seen firsthand what these monsters can do...I don't wish that on anyone. So if you have a plan, we should talk about it."

"The last plan I had nearly got us killed," I said. I slumped down onto the sofa next to Hope and let my head fall lazily onto her shoulder.

"No," said Jhamal, "your plan kept my aunt and me from being killed. I saw the ruthlessness that Warlock has. Do you think he's sitting back on his laurels somewhere waiting for you to make a move? Doubtful. Whatever they were planning, they are moving forward with it. Now."

"I hate to say it, but the kid is right," said Aunt Lena. We all knew she was joking. Out of everyone she had taken an immediate liking to Jhamal and the term "kid" was her way of ribbing him. "The eclipse is less than two weeks away. We still don't know anything about how the Warlock will go about creating this Leveling spell, let alone how to stop it."

I shuddered on the inside at the mention of the spell. The Warlock believed that it was possible, with the right magic, to halt the eclipse, creating a permanent night over the town of Trinity Cove. If he succeeded, his master, the vampire known as Mallis, would have free reign over this town. And since this town was sitting on top of a veritable gold mine of innate magical elements that flowed freely throughout the bedrock, he would be able to unleash a supernatural apocalypse; a new Hell on Earth.

But that wasn't going to happen. Not on my watch, at least. As Reliquary, I was able to store vast amounts of magic and use it at my will. Surely there was a way to stop this madness from happening. But right now, I couldn't think about any of that—the timer in the kitchen had just buzzed, and I jumped up and ran inside.

The smell in the kitchen was divine, and I knew that as soon as I opened the oven door, the aroma would waft outside and set everyone's tastebuds on fire. I carefully picked up the baking sheet with the ramekins arrayed on it. The soufflés were golden, high, and light. Perfect set. I couldn't wait to get them dusted with powdered sugar and covered in orange liqueur topping.

And, as luck would have it, that was when the warning alarms attached to the wards that protected the house went off.

I felt the brush against my skin. It was like someone had just taken a hairbrush out of the freezer and applied it to my scalp. The soufflés deflated like Tom Brady's football when I dropped them on the island.

"Damnit!" I said as I ran out onto the deck. Aunt Lena and Aunt Vivian, the only others in the house that could have felt the warning, were already looking out over the deck railing.

"What is it? What's going on?" asked Hope, moving away from the three of us. Fear played across her features. She had been around the occult long enough to know when something was about to go down.

"Something just set the wards off," said Aunt Vivian, not taking her eyes off the tree line at the back of our property.

We looked out over the backyard, focusing on the wooded area behind the house. It was getting dark, making it hard to see what exactly was out there.

"Hope, take Gar back into the house," I said. I summoned a small bit of magic and held it at the ready. Judging from the buzz in the air, my aunts were doing the same.

Before Hope—or more likely Gar—could protest, I felt it again. Only this time, the hit on the wards was harder and far more deliberate. It'd definitely come from the back perimeter.

"Got it," said Aunt Lena. "I recognize that creatures bio-signature."

"Indeed," replied Aunt Vivian, glancing over at me. "Vampire."

The Return of the Witch: Chapter One

"Stay here and protect Gar and Hope," I said to my aunts. "Jhamal, you're with me."

Jhamal nodded, and in the blink of eye he shifted into his lion form. The deck boards creaked under his weight as he padded over to stand next to me. I wrapped a bunch of his golden mane in my hand as he leapt over the railing. In midair I swung my leg over his back so that when he made contact with the ground I was sitting astride him. Together, we moved down the steep slope of the backyard towards the line of trees.

"Can you see him?" I asked.

Jhamal only nodded his large head as he walked purposefully towards a shadowy figure standing behind a massive pine tree. The thought of approaching a vampire after having gone through what I had only a week earlier caused my magic to flare protectively around us. I reached out with my mind, probing for more signatures that might tell me how many vampires there actually were. But his was the only *ping* I received from my mystical sonar.

Only one vamp. For some reason, that made the bloodsucker even scarier.

"I am alone," came a voice from behind the branches of the tree. Jhamal stopped about twenty feet away, and waited.

"Come out where we can see you," I said. There was some rustling of the branches, but no real movement. "Fine." I cast a ball of magical light into the air above the tree and willed it to luminesce outward. The vampire held up one arm to shield his eyes from the light and stepped forward, away from the shadows.

"I'm not here to hurt anyone," it said. "My name is Elion and I am not here to fight."

He stood away from the trees, stopping mere inches from the invisible ward that snaked around our property. The blue light from my magic illuminated him clearly and allowed me to make out most of his features. He was startlingly pale, with neatly-cropped dark hair atop a thin, angular face dominated by black eyes. Not just the pupils, or even the irises were black—the entire orbital structure was black, with tiny flecks of molten gold that danced in the darkness. He was slender of build, dressed in well-fitting jeans and a long-sleeved, light blue t-shirt. The shirt was stained with dark patches splattered across the chest and down the entire right arm.

Jhamal growled menacingly at the vampire—I didn't need him to tell me that the creature was covered in blood. Throwing one leg over Jhamal's back I slipped down off the great lion and walked over to the vampire. I stopped just before I reached the ward. To my magically-enhanced senses, it looked like a glowing blue wall with sparks of lightning spiderwebbing throughout. I trusted that the vampire would not be able to reach—or more importantly, bite—through.

Sensing Jhamal's discomfort, I waved reassuringly at him. Nonetheless, part of me was pleased to see the tension in the Lion-Shifter's body; he was prepared to attack at the first sign of any aggression from the creature that stood before us. The vampire looked over at Jhamal, taking in his massive form with those emotionless black eyes.

I sent a thread of magic through the ward and wrapped it around the vampire, probing for anything that might be… off. Not that I knew quite what to look for—just the fact that he was a vampire was enough to give me a serious case of the willies. But I figured that maybe my magic would pick up on any weird mystical weapons he might be hiding, or any truly evil intentions. Satisfied, I addressed him in the most non-shaky voice I could muster.

"What are you doing here?"

He took a deep breath, which surprised me. I didn't think vamps breathed, being dead and all.

"I need your… help." His voice was deep, but strained, his wording uneven.

Despite myself, I burst out laughing. "My help? How stupid does your master think I am?"

"I have no master, young witch." What I said must have sparked something in him; his eyes seemed to blaze a little more to life, and a hardness crept into his voice that caused a chill to race up my spine. "I'm sorry. I didn't mean to… put you off. But no one commands me."

"Tell you what. I'll give you one minute to say whatever it is you need to say, and if I'm not satisfied with it you're going to fry.. What do you think about that?" I hoped my bravado was enough to scare him off. Truth was, I still didn't know how to kill a vampire. But I was the only thing standing between this one and my family, so if it came down to it, I would light his ass up like a Christmas tree. I summoned fire and held it at the ready in the back of my mind.

The vampire didn't flinch, just locked those dark eyes on me while he spoke. "I need your help because I am being hunted. I want no part of what Mallis has planned for your community. And this town is only the beginning. When Mallis brings eternal darkness here, do you think he plans to stop? No, it will spread, engulfing everything in its path. It will be like a plague of locusts, locusts with sharp claws and hungry fangs that will devour everything in their path."

"The Leveling? I know what he has planned for us. It will require big magic. Magic that he doesn't have."

"You are wrong. Why do you think he has not come after you in the past few days?" He looked around and gestured at the ward separating us. "Do you think this would stop him?"

He caught me off guard with that one. I didn't have an answer, but I certainly wasn't about to let him know that. "Yeah. I do."

"False bravado, little witch. But whatever helps you sleep through the night."

Annoyance began to dance around in the back of my mind, and I decided it was time to move this along. "Tick tock *little* vamp," I said. To drive the point home I summoned a flare of magical fire into my hand and held it out in the bloodsucker's direction.

"Fine," he said holding up one hand as if in surrender. "As I said, I'm not here to fight. I couldn't even if I wanted to...Mallis believes he no longer needs you to bring about the Leveling. That is why he has not atacked."

"There haven't been any reports of kidnappings or

disappearances lately. He doesn't have enough witches to power the spell."

"He doesn't need them. He has taken a mate. A witch, and from what I've seen, she is powerful enough on her own."

My stomach churned at his words. Since I don't have balls, I can't really say what it would feel like to be kicked in them, but I think this was probably close. "That's a lie. No witch would betray her kind by doing this."

"Well, one of your type doesn't see that way. I have never met her; only Mallis is allowed to interact with her. Well, he and that Warlock of his. They are always locked away, practicing their magics. From what I have gleaned she is teaching the Warlock and improving his skills in the mystic arts. She is helping him prepare for the Leveling."

I took a slight step forward, not bothering to hide the anger in my eyes. "And how do you know all of this?"

"I was Mallis's…lieutenant at one point. Many years ago, before all of this. He sent for me a few weeks ago, and asked me to resume my position in his new movement."

"So then why are you here? Isn't there supposed to be some type of honor among thieving bloodsuckers?"

He winced visibly at that one, but continued on without missing a beat. "I am not the vampire I once was , said Elion, "the vampire Mallis remembers. When I was a newborn, I was dark and savage. I was a product of my times; easily molded into Mallis's image. But that was long ago, before Mallis left our home for these shores. In the ensuing centuries I have changed. I am not what he remembers, and when I refused to revisit such black memories, he turned on me. Or, more precisely, *she* turned on me, and convinced him I was a threat to his plans."

Something about the way he stood, the way he moved,

made me take a closer look at him. He wasn't standing up completely straight, and though he was visible in pockets of shadow created by my magical flare, I could see that he held one arm across his midsection.

"What's wrong with you?" I was practically right up against the ward and didn't dare cross through it to where he was standing for a closer look.

"After awhile, when Mallis couldn't convince me to join him, and his witch whispered in his ear that I was a threat, he tried to have me taken out. He threw me to his pack of wolves. I had to fight my way clear, and headed to the one place I hoped I could find help: here."

I cocked my head to one side, still eyeing him suspiciously. He responded to my distrust with a nod, then lifted his shirt to reveal long, jagged slashes across his torso. Cuts that were so deep I could see the white flesh beneath the muscle that was torn away. He then turned his back to me, showing deep puncture wounds in a semicircular pattern around his waist and lower back. Wolf bites.

With a wince, he faced me and lowered his top. He started to undo his belt but I stopped him. "No need to show me whatever happened down there. Why aren't you dead?"

"I'm not that easy to kill. But the wounds are very bad; I need to heal. The wolves will be out looking for me once the sun comes up. They know I will have to go to ground somewhere during daylight, I'll be defenseless and weak. That's when they will finish me off."

"So what, they follow you here and take all of us out in the process?"

"You are off-limits to attacks. At least for now," he replied.

"Why? I thought you said Mallis didn't need me anymore."

"I have no idea," said Elion, " but I do know that was an order that was given to the shifters. Perhaps he has back-end plans for you after the Leveling? Who knows. But that is why I came here. The wolves will not try to attack me at night...even wounded, I am still stronger than them. But the daylight is a different matter. No matter where I go, their senses will allow them to track me."

"Why aren't you healing? I thought that was what vampires do."

"I will. In time. But I can't take another mauling from the shifters. Mallis saw what happened to me. He knows I'm not dead."

"Then if he doesn't know where you are now, he will once the shifters track you tomorrow. They will track you right to my doorstep."

"Perhaps. Unless...a witch were to magically cover my trail. Or another type of shifter were to move through the woods in this area, masking my scent with his own very... unique one." He eyed Jhamal once again and received a warning growl in response.

"How are we supposed to trust you? What if I let you onto our property and you decide to go all uber-predator on us and take us all out?"

"I can only give you my word that I have no interest in being that person. As I said, I have changed. Besides, in my current condition I don't think I could survive an attack from your friend there. If it makes you feel better you could simply tether me."

"Tether?"

Now it was the vampire's turn to cock his head in my direction, raising one eyebrow. "You have a lot to learn. And

I will be happy to help you." He could tell I wasn't convinced. "Mallis fears you. I know that much. I can help you to learn about your magic and how to use it against the supernatural creatures that he is calling on, the creatures he is using to lead his charge into the new dark age he longs for. I have lived for over a thousand years, and in that time I have learned a thing or two about magic."

I looked him over again, and he really did look like he was at un-death's door. "How many wolves attacked you?"

"Six," he replied. "They were fast and vicious. Well-trained, they worked as a unit. They were all littermates." He raised his head and sniffed the air. "One has already been here, I see. His scent is all over you."

"What?"

"Whoever you have been with recently is a wolf. And from his scent, I can tell that he is a littermate to the band that serves Mallis now."

Grab your copy...
vinci-books.com/returnofthewitch

About the Author

M.J. Caan is an avid reader and writer of all things science fiction and fantasy. Author of multiple science fiction and paranormal fantasy series, M.J. likes to think that there is still magic out there in the world. Even if it's only between the pages of a great book.

www.ingramcontent.com/pod-product-compliance
Ingram Content Group UK Ltd.
Pitfield, Milton Keynes, MK11 3LW, UK
UKHW040923100426
469759UK00003B/43